Items should be returned on or before the last date shown below. Items not already requested by other borrowers may be renewed in person, in writing or by telephone. To renew, please quote the number on the barcode label. To renew online a PIN is required. This can be requested at your local library.
Renew online @ **www.dublincitypubliclibraries.ie**
Fines charged for overdue items will include postage incurred in recovery. Damage to or loss of items will be charged to the borrower. ADULT FICTION

Date Due	Date Due	Date Due

D0767730

Also by Sean O'Reilly

Curfew and Other Stories
Love and Sleep
The Swing of Things

Watermark

Sean O'Reilly

The Stinging Fly Press

A Stinging Fly Press Book

Watermark is first published simultaneously in paperback
and in a clothbound edition in May 2005.

The Stinging Fly Press
PO Box 6016
Dublin 8
www.stingingfly.org

Set in Palatino

Printed by Betaprint, Dublin

ISBN 0-9550152-1-9 (paperback)
0-9550152-0-0 (clothbound)

my hand between my legs
cover you with my wet warm pulse
feel how high I am
then my silent lips suck you til
you float back down

Graffiti. Dublin 2005

IT MUST BE HIM.

there is a black shining limousine parked in the street. It has to be him come back. Holding on to her hair, and wrapping her other arm around her waist, Veronica hurries herself along the pavement, her eyes on the ground, on her new green pointed cowboy boots he's never seen pounding the sunken pavement, the slippery cobbles and then the pale speckled slabs outside the new houses.

goes past the taxi office, the butchers which hasn't opened again since the robbery, the dry cleaners, the short row of houses with the white sentry box porches, sees herself reflected among the cartoon animals in the window of the new crèche, and then Anna's, which to her surprise is completely empty, not a sign of anybody watching and sniffing among the dusty shelves or even Anna knitting on her stool. The inside of the shop is dark, and the dark is cruel and ugly and unlucky, so ugly, and her heart shrinks at the sight of it

shrinks afraid away for a moment, vanishes, and she feels lighter suddenly than she has in weeks. Like she has forgotten everything with one quick glance into the silent shop. Maybe there's been an accident or a fight she wonders but she doesn't have time to stop or think she has to keep going, there is a limousine waiting for her, a long shining black car with silver buckles. And anyway, there's a good chance he has invited Anna and the rest of them back to the house for a drink to celebrate his return, that would be like him, so like him.

his return

it must be him

firebranded verdigree cowboy boots up to my knees in leather

With a leap, she leaves the pavement and runs toward the old tree, my lovely my lonely tree, the sole tree on the street with its long pale flaky trunk and the dirty bench underneath the twisted branches. She leans into the shadow breathes it in

the rank bitter musk stink mixes her up into a bloody compost dizziness

and the dirty gaudy bench sparkling with the curses carvings and drawings and inlaid names and promises overflowing onto the ground like an embroidered sheet like a dream coat left out to dry

Carol is a slapper gangbang Kev homo slag cunt bitch wanker get you back dead meat gives head multicoloured dick misspellings get you back love molester gives gives

suck my cock

riot randy slapper

From behind the window of the limousine, he will be watching her running towards him through the so graceful cold sunlight. His name is almost in her mouth floating up from the bloodless silence where she had imprisoned it.

Martin. Your face my watermark.

the smiling silver bumper, the whole sleek black body of the car gleams and shimmers like it might disappear if she is not fast enough, or she makes a mistake, if she stumbles or makes a show of herself.

She realises now that this was how she wanted it done—with style, with flair. Afraid to let herself hope, she must have dreamed it this way. Dreams come true my love. The engine of the car hums agreement and the sweet lilac smoke billows out from under the wheels beckoning.

Hurry yourself girl.

A few steps short of the car, she stops to catch her breath. There is not a soul on the street. The brown terraced houses are gathered to show her the way. She can hear the gulls above the covered market. Her mouth is so dry she won't be able to kiss him. A leaf falls next to her, still green with life, and she has a feeling she should pick it up and treasure it forever. Fluffing her hair, she takes a proud step towards him, mad with forgiveness.

Here I am my love.

The door will open and he will be there in the dark interior, smiling at her sleepily, stroking the soft leather seat. The place where she will sit.

Slowly, very slowly, like from a great depth, she starts to see her own reflection rising to the dull black surface of the window.

She waits for the door to snap like a twig. For the frozen black window to melt and reveal her future. She is smiling to show him that her love is as strong as ever.

Smile Veronica. Show him.

The delay must be because he's looking to play, wants to watch her waiting beyond the window. Pressing her hands hard against her hips, she pushes out her chest as raunchily as she knows how, pouts sullenly and gives him her profile which he used to say was regal.

that time dancing for him not letting him touch her while she twirled and stretched in a corset against all the furniture tantalising the table the walls chairs stroking the lamp stand and they came alive under her touch and crowded round her and she pretended there were others watching too and she could see them the men at their tables the smoke hear their voices and how she favoured him

who do you favour most

Up the street there, was that a face at the door of Anna's shop, that flash of movement. She would love Anna to come out now

3

and witness this moment. Anna has had to listen to her all these weeks and months. She wishes the men would step into the street and see her. Watch and learn what is possible. This is deeper than dreams. They never believed her.

Martin, she half cries eventually.

He is in there, getting hard on the back seat. The car remains silent as a sealed box. A black gift. Her reflection in the window is bothering her now—there's something about it not quite like her—it seems older, her hair longer. Is my hair too long heavy. She doesn't like it anymore. Standing there on the street.

Martin.

and reaches out to try the door handle, her smoky red nails inches from the unsmudged silver, a scratch away. Then, without knowing why exactly, on an impulse, she withdraws her hand and walks on. Let him follow her.

Martin, please don't ruin it.

He was always playing tricks on her. He made her laugh more than anybody else. That time he was telling her the story, some story, she wasn't really listening—it was just his face, his clean mouth and the happiness in his eyes—and she took him by the hand and pulled him into the bedroom before he had finished. He tried to be annoyed that she wasn't listening to him, he pulled his hand free, but she didn't care, I didn't care, I just wanted him inside me.

inside her

his mouth always so clean, the soft long lips, eyes of shell-blue light, a shell half buried in white sand, like the day he looked up at you from his tool box in the hall and you saw a boy, a real boy, all wonder and hope and no cynicism or distaste, blinking, fluttering all over your skin

inside you like a secret

how can I ever keep this

LIKE HER OWN WARM SHADOW, the car glides almost level with her now. Veronica stops lifts her nose haughtily in the air to pretend she is affronted. Silently, the front window slides down, a solemn veil of glass, and a pair of black-gloved hands are gripping the silky steering wheel. For a moment she can't find the face, not until her eyes follow one of the hands up to the peak of a chauffeur's cap. The driver's mouth is talking to her below his sunglasses.

A man in his fifties with a new cinnamon tan, unperturbed by Veronica's best scowl. Too much tan, a slick smile. Sunglasses.

Voice: Excuse us for bothering you... but I have a gentleman in the back and he wants to know whether you would like to have dinner with him.

Her reply: A gentleman? Have you no shame? Approaching a lady on the street like this?

Please, don't be startled. The black glove reaches out the window towards her and she steps back.

Don't be alarmed. The gentleman was very taken with you there, along the street there. We apologise for the rudeness, approaching you like this. The gentleman couldn't help himself.

that the way he touches the bridge of his sunglasses is meant to hide a sly glance in his rear-view mirror. Grey sideburns, hat too small for him, not right somehow, but the artificial smile is well practised. Does he have a wife who helps him put it on in the morning, get it right in front of the mirror while she's fixing his tie. That's it, hold it there now, honey, up a tiny bit at the corners. You'll make them faint today.

the gloved hand, not a big hand, newish gloves, moist, now lies open, palm upwards, not far from her, like he is asking for money. He's done this before, she thinks, many times. She wonders what the glove feels like inside, if it's lined, if it's silk, if it's hot in there

Do I look like the type of woman who is so easily impressed by a fancy car?

He dips his head back, blows out his cheeks, a way to say he expected better of her than that, a more original rebuff. She wants to tell him she's doing her best, that it wasn't her idea to play this game.

Repeats, He was very taken with you there up the street.

The black hand turns the other way up and raises a finger.

He wasn't planning this. He saw you through the window.

How taken? she asks, delighted with the question. Tell me. I want to know. How taken was he?

the driver turns back to the little mirror slit.

This better be good, she adds, flashing her eyes at the back window and settling her hands on her hips again. This really better be good.

Down the street, the sun appears pouring along over the houses and the tree, racing towards her and the limousine. Then it is gone. Was that a face again at the door of the shop, a sly head keeping an eye whispering back to the ones inside.

the time of her waiting in a gloomy shop, the men at their watch, Anna and her table and three odd chairs, the hours of pain and dreaming wishing her heart would die… this is the end of it and my new heart has space for the entire world, for every colour and face, and every tear and every tree and dirty bench, what would be enough in a moment like this, vast hungry human heart, heaven falling and turning like a speck of dust in the sunbeam of her joy

Martin

the driver has taken off his glasses to see her better. Small plain grey eyes. Mr Everybody.

Voice: The gentleman says that before today he has never really understood what the poets meant when they said that beauty is truth and truth beauty. Before today.

Veronica studies the points of her cowboy boots, then a stationary cloud, all its whiteness and curves.

That's not bad now. It's very nearly, but try again. She grins triumphantly.

The driver remains expressionless. The other way down the street she searches for her bedroom window where she learned how to wait also, lying on her bed sending out messages to him, tightening tightening, learned how to pull him in towards her between her thighs wherever he was

The gentleman says he knows what you want.

Does he now? And what's that?

The driver tells her indifferently, He says you want to make yourself come true.

Veronica smiles closes her eyes.

He says you dream of making yourself come true.

MARTIN, OPEN THE DOOR NOW. This is the moment. Throw open the door and take me inside, take my hand as I bend to get in. Right now. Please don't overdo it.

WILL I EVER COME TRUE. She went straight through the house to the garden, rushing down the hall, through the kitchen, as if he might be out there instead, that she would see something there to wipe it away, her embarrassment. Or somebody else there to see her, to really see her.

but nobody nobody nobody tiny sky bushes rubbish in the

grass after a flood
    oh my god this is the place where I used to be and the pain
now
    is stronger than
    who I was
    stronger than me this ghost left here now nobody
    You made me so real. So horny and real.

EVERYTHING IS AS THEY LEFT IT a week ago... so long ago. The garden has already sunk its countless green claws into the rubbish. The grass seems to have grown so hideously long, nourished by the sprays of champagne bubbles, the spilled wine and beer, the blood. All traces of the dancing have disappeared, the twenty or thirty sets of feet. Her own feet had been bare that night. Even the bushes have sprouted more leaves and bend lower heavier towards the plates on the table

the dried blood and bone bits on the curling paper plates. The flies are digging in. She had gone barefooted.

spent a whole afternoon in town searching for the perfect paper plates and cups, a certain texture and sheen and flexibility for the plates and cups that had to be the right colour. All her excitement, all her joy and happiness—was this what happened when you wanted too much. Those silvered cups with their tiny purple stars now lie about in the tangled grass

squashed puckered mouths full of insects or one a spider has sealed with a web. The bluebells stand guard over a half-eaten pork bone and the slugs are too bloated to make it up the wall. A late wasp sucking blood from the bars of barbecue grill. The gnats swirling greedily. The little birds sharpen their beaks against the walls of the house, the windowsills. All her pretty flowers have vicious colours.

Is he in up there.

High at the back of the house, his window is filthy. One of the four panes is cracked. The curtains are closed, filthy as well, soiled nylon rags. But that tells her nothing. She hasn't ever seen them open. This one lives in the shadows. His heart is only fit for the darkness.

Are you in, devil Donal.

runs in again through the kitchen, across the floor boards of the hall, to the bottom of the stairs.

Are you here? Bastard.

I could tear you apart like meat from a bone. Coward and liar. This house of his is bad luck. Calm yourself down Veronica. She can't let go of herself screaming like she usually does why not why not. Because she might not stop. Wrapping her arms around the giant mushroom of coats hanging on the banister head, she lets herself cry, wail, she doesn't care how loud it is

Can you hear me?

hopes he hears her up there in his room and knows he will never find beauty or peace. Or his cold gloomy silence he likes to think is wisdom.

Or ever feel the mad love of a woman like her.

Do you hear me.

WITH A CUP OF TEA, Veronica sits in the garden and waits for the grass to eat her, the birds to peck out her eyes, the slugs to slide between her toes. The autumn is coming, the wind and storm and rain that were supposed to mark his return. The thick jelly summer heat has sprouted little tails and swam away, all her dreams turned into frogs lost in the mucky back lanes and hopping stupidly across the motorway.

Martin and her in bed on a weekday afternoon, Martin and her painting a room together, walking at night on a country road and the moon red, seeing his face every morning as he looks out at the weather, them by the fire, them by the sea, on a long drive in his van, the outline of him against the roaring sea and all the time we have

me dancing for him in front of the fire lifting my skirt at the back flapping giving him glimpses the wind shaking the windows baby

every little flower she had planted was a grave the white trumpet daffodils the purple clematis the lavender crocus snowdrops. Speedwell which had her own name and tiny happy blue flowers.

now the autumn is a fake an ugly scam

without the watermark of his face

so alone that if she had reached for the silver handle on the door of that limousine how long would it have been before anybody even thought about where she was or what had happened to her. She shivers. A man whistles a few gardens along. The fat wood pigeons in the trees are humming with contentment, louder and louder like they are going to burst with it. In the grass, she stares at the pale blue seat she remembers standing on during the party, raising a toast to Donal for letting her stay, for listening to her through the weeks of longing while Martin was away.

dead summer I am going to die

She had gone barefoot all through the party and when she got a splinter or thorn Donal had been the one to sit her down and with a candle inspect the sole of her foot. He held her ankle firmly near his long square jaw. The heat of the flame making threats to her soft skin. Had he already made the call by then. Had he already told Martin what had happened, even though she had forgotten all about it. While the flame whispered what it wanted to do to her and she laughed so loudly and he glided his coarse smoky fingers lightly up and down her sole looking for the tiny catch of the thorn, her ankle locked in his fist, had you already told him by then bastard.

she glares up at his window, the curtains the ugliness

and that seat, she had painted that blue seat herself, and the other three, and the round handmade table one afternoon shortly after she moved in. Martin was going away for three months and when he came back they were going to move out of the city, she didn't care where. It would be everything she wanted, her escape, the two of them together, completely together in their own rhythm. No more running around to the drums of the city, the dissatisfaction she could see stiffening her face. Or pointless conversations with people she didn't care about or nights in bars drinking for the sake of it, all those useless wasted words, trying to pretend this was the place to be and yet every day forgotten immediately. In the meantime, while Martin was gone, she would stay here in Donal's house, his best friend.

them in the kitchen, talking, as they always did, they talked for hours, nobody else could keep up

them in the kitchen and music on smoking their joints and cooking a roast. Smells of the meat and garlic and rosemary in the garden stirred in with the paint where she was kneeling on a newspaper doing the chairs, smearing them in pale blue. Her moving-in party although there was never much need of an excuse for those two to have a get-together and people to arrive. She was in a hurry to get the chairs done so they would have time to dry. They tried to persuade her not to bother there wouldn't be time but she had got it into her head, the image of those blue chairs in the candlelight in the garden had to come true. After all, the party was to celebrate her, and the time she would spend there, her waiting. She wanted it to look stunning, she liked to have beauty around her, she had said with a coquettish shrug that had surprised her and left the two men speechless for a moment, and to cover her embarrassment she had gone further and treated them to a rebellious shake of her hips as she stepped out into the wet garden happier than she could remember.

Happiness. She laid down some newspaper to protect the grass and started on the first chair, which she knew she should have sanded first to remove the rust and old paint. Wearing only her dungarees, and nothing else next to her skin; the dampness from the ground quickly spread through the denim to her knees. The sharp taint of the thick baby blue paint, the grass and dripping trees, and the warm oven aromas from the kitchen were the smell of the future. She breathed it all in. Everything was going to change. And she could hear Martin's low voice, the words so soft they flowed together, and she was inhaling that too as he was telling some story or other and then

then it went quiet. The birds were quiet, there wasn't a sound. She was sure they were both watching her, standing at the door watching her she could feel it. She sat back on her heels, holding the paintbrush. The strap slid down off her shoulder, her strong shoulder, her white strong shoulder. They were watching her in silence. She closed her eyes and straightened her back, stretched her neck.

my hair was pinned up. I could feel their eyes on me. My heart was so happy. I had been kneeling there all my life. It was wrong to turn around but I wanted to. I couldn't stop myself.

a drop of the blue paint fell on the fine grass, trickled down to the soil. It was so beautiful she gasped. She turned to call them, come here, look, but it was only him there, only Donal leaning in the doorway, his piercing glossy know-it-all black stare, only him who witnessed that moment.

IT WAS ONLY A KISS.

her mouth so dry and her lips burning and flinching with each sip of the cold yellow wine. He was coming back and she was glowing radiant, everyone could see it. Her hair was alive like its roots were deep in her heart. The wait was over. She had shown them the strength of her love.

it was only a kiss and yes, she was the one who had started it, yes, it was her who had opened his thin lips with her tongue, forced them open with her giddy tongue. Her mouth so dry.

she could have kissed a hundred men that night, she would have danced close to them, pounded them with her hips. She would have loved to dance a flamenco in a circle of men clapping, stamping her foot, throwing back her proud head, she would have moved among them hardening their eyes, swelling their groins, making them thirsty, and it would mean nothing. She was happy that's all. The flat copper sun was going down with long warm spokes of light in the grass under her bare feet. The smoke from the barbecue didn't want to lift and the clouds of midges scribbled all over the air

making remaking

like you could imagine it anyway you wanted

she danced all night couldn't stop in her bare feet and the vintage dress with the high waist under her loose breasts

The wait was almost over. She had made it through the lonely mornings and the restless nights, the constant grief that he wasn't there to share a moment with, a lovely meal, a rain shower, a walk along the giant wing of the pier… and the despair after the long telephone calls when she could hear the impatience in her own voice and couldn't control it and wanted to skip all the words

Martin guess what I'm doing now

when she had played with her own breasts for him, wet her nipples, her long nipples slipped out of her underwear and touched herself for him, imagining him there in the room, sitting in the chair, smoking, maybe a walking stick with a silver handle, a connoisseur of spectacles of women writhing alone on their beds, arched backs and moans, touching her with his cane raising her back opening her legs that bit wider, and then the tears afterwards and he wasn't there to hold her and tell her it was ok, she was beautiful, her hunger wasn't bad.

Don't be afraid of this Veronica. This is what's good.

Yes, it was her who had started it. She had danced into the kitchen and found Donal alone at the table, rolling another one of his joints. She laughed at him, bent over with her hands on her knees and blew the little white paper off the table to the floor. Pulled him out of his chair and made him dance with her. He was a terrible embarrassed dancer. He couldn't let go of himself. His long limbs were supple and fluid but he had no coordination so she kissed him instead and when she released him and saw the look on his face, his bleak confusion, her lipstick on his unshaven mouth, she had laughed and kissed him again with even greater passion. Martin her man was coming back to her in a few days time. Look at me: see how happy I am. See how beautiful the world can be.

Martin was away in the desert making a documentary, living in tents, eating around a fire with the tribes. She went to sleep at night imagining his face around a fire and the unblinking eyes of veiled women who watched his every move in secret. He was a good height, lean and strong with a feminine purity to his face that sometimes made him seem masked to her. His eyes were a childish open blue through the holes in the mask. They had met at a dinner party; she was there on a date with another man who she was realising was not the person she thought he was. Martin had only arrived back from a trip the day before and dominated the table with stories of his travels. He seemed to care about things other than himself, about the world. She thought he was gentle, sincere and fond of making fun of himself. She wanted him to look at her the way he sometimes stared at the posh woman next to her with her perfect cleavage and long pale arms. At the end of the evening she followed him upstairs to the toilet intending to say only that she had enjoyed his company and she believed they should keep in touch. It wasn't like her to act in this way but for some reason she didn't think of stopping herself or how it might look. She forgot to care. Outside the bathroom door, she listened to the sound of his pissing splashing a long torrent which might smell of the asparagus and the red wine he had been drinking, and how he hummed up and down through the scales, trying to get higher each time or lower into the baritone. Life was a game to him she thought wrongly then. He came out of the toilet doing up his belt.

the belt of cracked green leather the heavy brass buckle his perfect hairless fingers

he sat on the edge of the bed in one of the rooms said he wanted to see her breasts

she had stood there in front of him outside the toilet offering herself to him so freely

my breasts

he kissed her breasts and his tongue urged her nipples to grow circling them lightly like he understood quickly and toyed with them and she sighed for him and closed her eyes and stood there naked for him with the dress around her ankles and for minutes he must have been looking over every inch of her only looking and humming to himself so quietly

or counting down from the highest number

across the city all the boys at all the windows were counting down in unison with their heads out into the street as she stood there bared to him

until he surprised her with a touch of his lips at the bottom of her back plucked out of her a sweet blind never-ending note

as he circled her like a statue coming to life not a word and she was so wet she wanted to piss my body

my young body

my young body shivering crouched inside the big concrete

pipe in the field and the boys shouting out the numbers together from over at the hole in the wire fence. Twenty… nineteen… eighteen. This was my first time allowed to play, Cathy and me. I hoped she was in the next pipe but I didn't dare call for her to see. I was hunkered down, my little skirt pulled up over my knees. I was wearing pink sandals. Some of the boys had been in there before and written their names on the inside of the pipe and drawn some dirty pictures. Like the spine of an animal, a skinny tuft of weeds and moss ran in between my ankles and under my dress. Fifteen… fourteen… thirteen… All the girls had to find a place to hide. I wasn't sure what happened when one of the boys caught you. You weren't supposed to fight them when you were caught. You had to do whatever they asked. The big concrete pipes were left in the field after the estate was finished, and some had even found their way mysteriously deep into the wood. They were like the tubes in the hamster cage at school. I was too nervous to pretend to be a hamster. I wanted to pee. I heard a girl screaming but I couldn't tell who it was. Suddenly the counting stopped too early. The boys always cheated. Through the open end I could see the edge of the wood and a boy running, Jimmy with the crooked teeth. He wasn't the one I wanted to kiss. What would they do when they caught me. There were stories about what they did with their hands. I was going to pee myself with nerves. I couldn't hold it in. Running feet in the grass came nearer and a boy's breathing. What if I had to show him my knickers and they were all wet. Or he could smell it if I had to let him kiss me. No matter what I tried to think about to distract myself, the pee was trickling out of me so I let it go. The steam went up between my legs in a warm cloud. The moss changed colour and drank and drank and swelled up like it was coming alive. Then I heard a laugh. I looked round over my shoulder at the other end of the pipe which I had forgotten about and there was a boy laughing. My pee was flowing towards him in two smoking streams. I begged him not to tell.

Please don't tell. I was bursting.

He came into the pipe, balancing with his hands pressed against the side. His name was Darren. He was the one I was hoping for. He had cheeky green eyes and the others said he went into the wood with the older girls. I made him promise not to tell. Smiling like he knew more about promises than I did, he was right up close to me and knelt down and didn't care about the stains in his trousers.

SHE WAS GOING FROM ROOM to room in the house and each one of them was completely changed; there was new furniture of leather and glass, expensive tweed curtains and surprising colours on the walls—the fireplace in the living room had been bricked over. A tall woman with long ghostly hair who showed her around talked about the house and who had lived in it, mentioned their names, Martin, Donal, but not her own. Veronica went to the window and saw a naked child in the garden pulling a balloon out of the ground. The woman was hinting that there had been some catastrophe in the house. The awful thing was the redecoration was a success; in every room, including what used to be her own bedroom, Veronica had to admit the modern furniture, the colours and contrasting textures, even the painted floorboards made much more of the space than she had done and that all the work she had put into the house was clumsy, hurried, bland and tacky. She was so ashamed of herself.

I used to live here too you know.

Wrapped in a blue cashmere blanket from the back of the sofa, she rushes up the bony uncarpeted stairs and knocks on his door. His door with the deep straight split in the wood you can nearly see through. She shivers in the hall, in the dark stitched together out of strips and patches, smooth and rough fabrics, silks and horsehair

She had fallen asleep under the blanket on the sofa in the front room and had a dream.

knocks at the door again catching her knuckle in the crack in the wood. She curses gives the door a kick. He could be in one of his trances, his silences when he doesn't move for hours and his eyes are inhumanly empty. On a few occasions she went into his room and found him sitting on a round embroidered cushion on the floor. He was staring at the candles in front of the little fireplace in which he kept a picture of a black jagged mountaintop. Sometimes he had his drum on his lap, stripped to his underwear. He had a lot of dark hair on his chest like a coat of arms. Pale skinned, he looked better built without his clothes, firmer, less indifferent. She would say his name and get no response. Usually she left him alone.

Are you here.

opens the door and only then remembers all that has happened. She used to tell him so much. He made her feel proud of her own complexity, that she shouldn't be afraid of it. She even told him about her dreams. She trusted his silence, the torment he seemed to be in. The night before the party she had dreamed that Martin was dead. Guiltily, she went straight to tell Donal first thing in the morning, sat on the edge of his bed. He took her hand and told her not to worry

said the Martin who had died was the one who had stayed beside her to keep her company and now the job was done.

That smell of his like biscuits, the oatmeal crumbs of a biscuit tin, in the dark of his room, on his towels, his clothes. Her nails scratching the wall, she finds the light switch she knows is above the old ivory globe of the world that doesn't turn anymore. He's not there. She can't go to him and tell him things anymore. He's ruined it all. Everything is ruined. Treacherous bastard.

She sits in his creaking revolving chair at the desk, wrapped in the soft blue blanket. That's his mother's bed against the wall, the place where she died, flowing chestnut brown carved wings and legs and a high headboard with two spears. This is his mother's house and the place he grew up in. All his toys are in boxes in the attic. The garden shed is packed with her rotting furniture. The rest of the room is bookshelves, like a rib cage stuffed with books and paper. Padding to keep the draught out. Peacock feathers stuck in the soil of a dead plant. A broken accordion in a corner like a grotesque jewel. And that horrible skull with its horns on the bedside table, a fake, invented, a wolf's head with two curved white horns. Biscuit smells and smoke and dead books, the odour of a bleak cruel man. It makes her want to take off her clothes, to expose her breasts in defiance.

Donal is tall and turbulent and vicious. His dark looks are more supernatural than human. He is either summoning the ghost of some misery in his room or he disappears for days on end and returns with an arrogant glee in his eyes. Martin is softer finer and though he would never admit it, he's afraid of Donal, agrees too easily with every tortured absurd thought that comes out of his friend's mouth. Martin is gentler cleaner like a thin line of sunlight across the floor. It's all intellectual for them anyway. They talk and talk like they think they are doing the world a favour. At the start, it used to excite her.

I used to love listening to them, watching their hands and eyes, their thirsty mouths, I couldn't wait to get Martin into bed and show him what was inside me. I wanted him to talk about me in the same way he talked about his politics and books, for him to get as furious with me, as disappointed and excited, to imagine me with the same passion as he thought about the future and how everything should be. I wanted to be the founder of the fairest society, the first girl he ever kissed, the winter evenings when his father read to him, the violent collapse of capitalism, the steering wheel of his red van, his mother's breast, the sun in his eyes, a new CD he liked, his box of tools and screws and wire, the words pouring constantly out of his mouth.

Before the three of them met for the first time, Martin warned her that Donal could be difficult to handle. He told her that Donal used to be a travel writer, that he had been all over the world, to the strangest most remote places. A publisher had given him money to write a book about his adventures. In Siberia or somewhere like that, or maybe it was Mongolia, he had gone on a journey with an old man. Martin said he came back changed, nervous, broken, violent, and that he had given up writing the book. It was impossible to get the full story out of him, only bits and pieces to do with drugs and some kind of shaman person. A spirit got hold of him, Martin said, and she had laughed in his face. A spirit demon and drugs. It sounded ridiculous to her. Pathetic. Although she promised not to say a word, it was almost the first thing she said to him when they met in that cellar bar.

So I hear you're possessed.

Donal glared at Martin ferociously. Kicking back his chair, he stood up. Martin tried to placate him. Veronica laughed at the pompous fool. When he had gone, Martin was like a deserted child; he couldn't help himself and ran out after his friend. Veronica was left there by herself in that ugly pub for a quarter of an hour before the two of them came back.

Even then, he barely looked at her. He was humourless and extremely arrogant, spoiled. He sneered at everything. She didn't like him. How could Martin talk so warmly about this sullen self-pitying man with his square shaved skull and his annoying mixed-up accent, a man who could have been handsome and even graceful, a hopeless grace. With grimy rings on his long stained fingers. How could she possibly share a house with him, see him every morning, eat with him, be herself around him without losing her temper. Now she was the one about to walk out of the pub. Martin took her hand under the table. He knew what she was thinking. But what choice did she have. She had nowhere else to go now. So she said to him straight out, to Donal, as soon as they were left alone,

I trust Martin. He has a high opinion of you. I have to hope what he's told me about you is true but to be honest with you I don't see it at all.

He lifted his eyes to her for the first time, they were dark and cloudy, misty like the way grapes go, grapes about to burst, deep in a taut stern face.

I trust Martin as well, he said, but that doesn't mean he's always right. About me or anything else.

She took the hint; it was her he meant.

I suppose you think you know better than everybody?

The less I know the better I feel, he said so mournfully it repelled her.

I don't believe that for a minute. And she added, Or that you believe it either. It sounds to me like words you've learned off.

He shrugged, met her with a hard patronising stare. Do you actually think you can see inside me, it said. She was about to bring it to his attention that he might not be as hard and profound as he would like to think when the hard stare melted away suddenly and he smiled, a weak resigned smile, and shrugged again.

Maybe you are right, he said in another strange accent, maybe this is meant to be. I shouldn't resist it. For good or bad.

What?

I don't know what I think these days. I used to be very sure. When I went outside there, I found this ring on the street, he said laying it on the table.

a plain gold band with a missing stone

Not so long ago I would have thought this was a sign, that it had some meaning I had to understand. But now, he took the ring from her and dropped it in the ashtray, I don't know anymore. In fact, the idea that it might have a meaning makes me feel sick.

He looked at her now, peered into her face, waiting.

Veronica took the ring out of the ashtray, wiped it clean on her skirt and put it back in front of him on the table. He pushed it back towards her, smiling, a warmer smile which she returned.

I don't want it, she said.

He shrugged, reached for his pint.

People think too much about things they can't do anything about, she said and she knew it was automatic, to do with nervousness.

And where did you learn that one off? he laughed, and she found herself laughing with him.

a ring without a stone

she often thought about it, the look they gave each other as they left the pub that day, the shared tarnished conspiracy, him holding the door open for her, the ring left behind on the table, and how outside on the street blue-eyed Martin asked her what was so funny and only then she realised they had not mentioned it to him, that he hadn't even noticed the ring,

and she had thrown her arms around him kissed him hard and Donal was wandering on by himself along the street, his hands clasped behind his back

that self-satisfied walk she hated to behold in a man.

THE FIRST NIGHT AFTER MARTIN had left, Donal surprised her by asking if she would go to the cinema with him. Happy to be alone, happy to pine and dream in her bed, she tried to refuse but he had made a promise to look after her and wouldn't give up. His loyalty softened her towards him. He must be missing Martin too, she thought.

They left the film before the end, they'd been too late for the one they wanted to see, and walked around the city centre without being drawn into any of the bars or cafés. There was a pink sky gulls laughter all the way along a cash point queue and the bars were noisy and cheap with gangs of girls she was happy not to be a part of. He offered his arm and she took it. She liked to walk arm in arm with a man, not hand in hand. Outside a restaurant they happened to meet someone he knew, and then more people on another street and she noted how each one of them was delighted to have run into him and listened to him closely. When he introduced her she felt not only that they assumed she was with him but from their smirking patronising expressions that he was often with a woman, that she was one of many. She tried to tease him about it afterwards, and he turned on her, said those people knew nothing about him, that she had no right to judge him. Veronica walked off. He caught up with her and apologised.

They walked all the way back to the house. It was the very beginning of summer, the streets had been there for centuries. She talked to him about her childhood, the long months off school, about the feeling of going to bed dirty from the streets and the field. About the smell of herself as a girl. He said very little, told her that her name meant the moment when the matador pulled the cape away from the horns of the charging bull. He stooped slightly forward from his shoulders. She sat in the big ragged deep armchair in his room and he filled her lap with books to keep her busy while her lover was away.

his gloomy and dusty room with the biscuit tin smell. He moved around languidly or stood away in the shadows, never sitting down. Reappearing to place the ashtray and joint on the arm of the chair, blowing the smoke down his nose like an angry animal. He was silent and talked a lot, that's how she felt. She wasn't sure if she was saying too much or being dull and boring.

Although he asked her a lot of questions he seemed to be the one always talking. His head was shaved short all over, a straight line across the broad worried forehead and deep-set dark dewy eyes

it was the wet dark grape eyes about to burst and split open with sorrow. He was sad and muscular and agitated and angry. She pitied the woman who would love him.

all his stiff words in the room with the slow grey smoke. His mother's deathbed. The round drum lying on his mother's bed where he'd thrown it after giving up trying to explain, the skin it was made from, the meaning of the symbols. So stoned, it was hard to understand him. She could never remember the conversations she had with people anyway. Were they talking about his mother or Martin or the house or something else now. The words people say aren't the important thing. They're just part of the mood, like birdsong or smoke in a stranger's room

the smoke said more or the sternness when he's listening or how he scratches his arms talking or the way he crosses his legs or the sorrow in his eyes

he threw a party almost every weekend during that summer. She met so many new people. She waited.

IN HIS BIG CHAIR by the fireplace she told him all about the fox. It was after he'd told her out of the blue, rushing towards her with his arms out, falling to his knees by her chair

like he was in a fit

about one summer when his aunt came to stay and what she made him do to her, what she showed him how to do in the room where Veronica was sleeping. His story had turned her on. His fear and the way he made it sound cursed honoured and inevitable

take this cup from me

YOU WERE TWELVE and it was summer, a long restless summer day. You went out into the fields around the estate lay down on your stomach in the dry yellow grass. You had butterflies in your stomach but all there was to look at was the car wrecks the concrete pipes the broken trees and even the sun was an old tired thing. Every scratch on your legs stung and burned from the week away in the caravan where you had met that boy from the north carrying the triangular cartons of milk leaking behind him on the road. Where was he now would he write to you would you ever see him again. You were so glad to have a secret. You wanted more and more secrets. A forest of secrets behind a high wooden gate. A golden key so big you kept it in a violin case. Lying there, shredding and weaving grass stalks, you saw Wobbles get up on top of a car and begin to batter the roof in with a stick. If you closed your eyes the noise was sad like somebody trying to say they were sorry over and over again. Poor Wobbles, he had some problem with his balance and a face full of sore red freckles. You ran over to him in your yellow shorts.

ordered him to follow you and led him round and round the car through the dusty grass and round another car climbing in and out through the windscreen, through a pipe and on into the trees. Led him across the fallen trunk over the green sticky stream weaving between the trees and into the brambles and anticlockwise round some more trees. He would have followed you forever and you wanted him to, poor unhappy Wobbles who nobody ever played with, you were going to let him kiss you and then have him follow you again until you found another spot to let him kiss you, the right tree, the right smell, the right colours to show him what you had learned at the caravan from the northern boy.

by the stream again just as you were about to jump, you saw the fox lying in the grass oozing bubbling blood with each quick breath. It had long legs and a white neck. Wobbles battered it with his stick before you could stop him. He had the blood of it on his hands and clothes. Then he picked it up and chased you with it. The guts were hanging out of it. He caught you and wanted something not to smear it all over you.

he didn't know what he wanted

held it by the ears by the tail over you it's sharp bleeding teeth the snout kissing you

wanted you to take off your shorts and then your knickers and show him.

laughing he held the fox over you and let it drip on your stomach running down between your legs so warm and black red

he put his bloody fingers all over inside you

cut off the tail with his penknife and tickled you with it

The next day all the boys were sitting on the wall outside her house when she came out. They all stared at her strangely. Nobody said a word. They followed her to where the fox should have been. They dug and kicked hunted for ages in the grass while she knelt there in her green frock weaving a cross out of the reeds. One of them had a knife but all he did was throw it at the trunks and it never stuck. One took a long piss behind a tree. They started fighting among themselves. Another less shy one started pissing in the grass near her and tried to get some on her for a joke. That started them all off and every one of them opened their flies and aimed at her as she rolled around in the grass like she was a fox herself or some animal they were lashing with their green and yellow whips. Foxy they called her after that. They wrote it on the walls. Foxy Gives Foxy is a Slapper Slut Whore Sucks Cocks

The older boys looked at her more.

Foxy Veronica Ronnie the Fox.

DONAL DIDN'T EVEN LAUGH as she told him, he seemed almost pained by it, like a priest would have been, pained and amazed and gratified at the same time.

She had never told this to a soul before, thought she had forgotten it.

I'm sorry, she said. I shouldn't have told you that.

Why not? He was standing behind her chair.

I haven't even told Martin.

Why not?

Veronica was silent.

Do you think he wouldn't like it? Donal asked as he moved in front of her. She looked up at his face in the smoke for a sign of treachery. As if to show his earnestness, he asked her the same question again.

I have to go to bed, she said. I'm dizzy.

Donal walked towards his fake skull on the table, lifted it and said, I'd like to hear more of your stories.

Who said I had any more?

He didn't answer.

Help me. I'm so dizzy.

He put the skull down, your fabrication

Your own myth

offered her his hand.

Don't tell Martin.

He agreed too readily as though he was admitting that Martin wouldn't like it. But she was too stoned then to find out if this were true or if she was being paranoid.

I never told you about the fox, Martin. I hadn't even begun to tell you so much. You left me in this state now. I thought I could show you.

You said it was ok you wanted it all.

THE MORNING IS MISTY and damp. She pulls a chair to the back door, drinks her tea looking out at the garden. Will today be the day. Does the city know. Will I ever look back on this moment or will it be forgotten. My hands around this cup. My hair up. The stiffness of my shoulders. A door open to the misty garden. The gulls

the gulls make her want to

wishing the day would stay insubstantial, that the shapes would fail to come out. That the gulls would cry all day for the loss of the world.

Wearing her new silk milky green dressing gown, ankle length, belted, that sits perfectly on her cleavage, bought for his return, she goes from room to room. Upstairs, the two bedrooms, the cold bathroom with the rust-stained sink and the small back room which is full of cardboard boxes and useless furniture. The stairs, she had taken the carpet up, sanded them by hand because they were so narrow and uneven, take her down to the living room, her pride and joy.

It was hard to believe now but after only a couple of days in the house she had started to redecorate. The place needed it and she felt she was giving something back for being allowed to stay there rent free. Donal said she could do whatever she wanted and she took him at his word. She cleared the living room first, her favourite room because of the old tiled fireplace, green and purple tiles with peacocks up either side, and told him he wasn't allowed inside until she said so. She could imagine herself waiting in front of the fire for her lover to come back and hold her. She stripped the paper, plastered, got the walls ready, sanded and varnished the floors, spent days looking for the right curtains, which she thought might be purple and flyaway but turned out to be a heavy blue velvet. She found some cheap bright rugs and painted the whole thing off-white.

the ashes in the fireplace were probably from the night of the party. Dirty glasses and cups on the floor by the window. The candles burned down into big warts. A mirror with its face to the wall. Carpet tassles. A three legged table and a lamp with a round paper shade. The blue blanket on the grey cord sofa, split in the middle. The walls. The window. These things were now more real than her. They were waiting. She had taught them to wait. Now they wouldn't stop. They would wait forever. They ignored her. She wasn't needed any longer. They didn't even know she was there.

I am a ghost.

In the next room along the downstairs hall, this was going to be her second job, the air reeks of white spirit

sting of pain. On an old yellow bed sheet the pots of paint like they've bubbled over and out under their lids and the brushes in wrinkled tins. Tins with their labels off. And an old chest of drawers with a saw in the top drawer. These are the rooms where she counted away the days

the palace of my waiting.

She had grown to love the wait, every moment, no matter what she was doing, hoovering the room, washing the dishes, looking at the dirty bench from her bedroom window or doing her toenails. Her hair pinned up still wet from the shower and moisturiser sweetening her skin, she might be waiting for the bread to hop up from the toaster, the sink stacked with dishes, the bin so full the lid won't fit on, rain clouds coming toward her over the houses and find herself thinking of him, that he wasn't there, he couldn't see her, that somehow he couldn't be there because of the fullness

there wasn't room for him

he would never know how the cold floor tiles were sucking the heat out of her body and how it was connected to the colour of the clouds and the dream from the night before and that there were no rings on her fingers and the heat rising from the toaster and the front door rattling in a gust of wind

to stand near the sink in the afternoon with one foot balanced on the other for warmth

how it changed the position of her hips her back her neck

and how suddenly fast her heart was beating like something was about to happen

and that she might be making it up

making him up

that her love was

and couldn't stop and there was nothing else and

Now his name smells of paint and varnish in an empty house. She lets a spoon fall from her hand to the kitchen floor, says her own name on the way up the dark stairs and knocks gently on her bedroom window at nothing. She decides to force herself to get dressed, humming to deafen herself to the noise of the coat hangers and even the rustle of her clothes. She is still naked when the door knocker startles her. For some reason she doesn't hurry. By the time she gets down, listening closely to every creaking footstep on the stairs, whoever it was has gone. The sound of the door when she closes it tells her more about loneliness. She can hear the traffic from the main road, two sirens plaited together. She expects to see herself at every window along the street, it wouldn't surprise her to run into herself coming out another door. She is going to see Anna.

Under the tree, she sits on the edge of the dirty bench shuts her eyes and inhales. Makes herself smell it, the gross smells, the rottenness, the mossy stink, the drink and piss searching for her own being at the heart of it, her own hunger.

He smelled of hills, she told him.

The way a bird would smell who lives high in the hill, a hawk, the breast of a falcon bird of prey heather.

No matter how early it is, there will always be one of them leaning among the empty shelves, staring out at the day through the door. The light that has to be studied for signs, the slant of the rain, wind direction, temperature, wind. The faces of the people who peer in or those that won't let themselves. The cavemen, he called them. Today there is Eyck, a small man with sores on his face who told her one day about his quest to find his daughter. And McGrory who is drunk already and chewing over his great disgrace. And there's quiet Teddy in his suit and tie who lost everything in a fire, his wife and family and his brother who was staying over for the night. Gravy is busy arranging the contents of his pockets on the shelves of the empty fridge.

It is different every morning; sometimes there can be a singsong going before the street has even gone to work and the reason is always secret or as Yen said, it's a jinx to talk about it. Or they might greet her warmly, welcome her in, surround her and grope tenderly at her hair and shoulders or they might ignore her altogether like this morning, sullen leering vicious, like she has let them down, the cans of beer on the shelves, smoking and spitting out the door, while Anna sits on her stool at the counter.

She'll take Veronica by the hand turn her around to get a good look at her and lead her into the back kitchen fill the kettle and say

I woke up thinking about you this morning sweetheart. This is your day I can feel it.

Her face is a shattering of fine lines although the skin still appears young. She has a young girl's chin. Her eyes are large but the green is far away like it is being kept in a box with a smudged glass lid. Comically, she has the crimson ears of somebody constantly embarrassed. Now in her late sixties, she wears nothing more than a plain grey pleated skirt and one of a number of shapeless cardigans. A small golden crucifix is her only decoration. The rare glimpses of her legs when she bends over in the kitchen show she has kept her figure. Once a flowing shining brunette maybe, her hair is now forgotten in a rigid greasy knot at the nape of her freckled neck. She is well spoken with full precise lips. Veronica thinks she is a woman who believed in beauty and then learned to scorn it. She lets the local drinkers use her shop for their long vigils. Years before, on a dreary spiteful afternoon, she let a few of them stand in out of the rain, the story went, and there they have remained.

They call it the grotto or the cave. The standing shelves are empty, maybe a bag of sugar, a few tins of peas or damp firelighters. In a cardboard box by the door, some loose potatoes onions carrots are on display like ancient shrivelled relics. Anna keeps some boxes of cigarettes in a drawer behind the counter and three jars of sweets for the children who never appear. The light comes from a single bulb in the hall to the kitchen and whatever sneaks in from the street.

Always full of smoke and drunks it was hard to see how she made any money. But maybe money wasn't the point, Veronica would remind herself, and anybody else who brought up the question. Money wasn't the point. The new families that had moved into the street used the late night place on the main road with security guards at the automatic door and a hot food deli counter, avoiding even the pavement outside Anna's with its hard stew of spit and butts and worse like they would step around blood spilled there. Donal told her the rumour in one of his filthy moods that Anna often took one of the men, Big Griffin, to bed with her, a man with long yellow white hair in a ponytail who had travelled the world on the boats, and when he wasn't around the others fought in the street over who would take his place. Veronica accused him of being vicious about other people. He could get like that; the world was evil and sick. Martin was more compassionate towards people.

Coming home one night along the street, she heard voices from the window above the shop, shouting, singing, Anna's laughter. She told Donal when she got in, talking to him through his bedroom door. Told him that she had knocked, and knocked harder to be let in.

Donal's door opened: You're not serious? You knocked?

She made a fist rattled her knuckles on his door to show him. Then for some reason she blew him a kiss. She went down to the kitchen. Sleep was far away. She was planning to think about Martin, maybe smoke a joint to heighten the pleasure. She wanted him to sit in the chair and watch her on the bed

but he's not allowed to come near, to touch, not until she says so. She had been imagining it all day, she had it planned out. Then she heard Donal's bare feet on the stairs. That became another night they sat up late talking. So much self-indulgent talk. He seemed to be trying to shock her with his stories about the women he had known. The stuffed tiger story. The hitchhiking sisters. The school girls with the gun. Drugs and sex. The story about Anna, about after her husband died.

and the boys used to stand in the lane behind the shop and watch her undress at the window and she knew

and some of them claimed she brought them upstairs and gave them drink and fags they swore and swore and one of them had a bit of her jewellery for proof a ring or something

THE BACK KITCHEN is a small damp yellow room. They sit at a little table covered in a summer-blue plastic cloth which sticks to whatever touches it, the saucers, the hotel ashtray, the plates, her elbows, on two unmatching chairs. There is a barred window behind a clean net curtain and a tiny door that leads upstairs. Anna washes out the pot puts in the bags fills it with boiling water

and sets it on the table. Brings the cups and saucers and a plate of biscuits, and the little striped blue milk jug from the fridge with its sweet tiny lip

Veronica covets its delicacy makes her eyes brim with tears.

You have your cry sweetheart. Is there no word from him then?

There won't be. There never will be. I ruined it. I ruin everything. Now I've nothing left. Anna, my heart is dying. It's so sore. I'm having these dreams that are wearing me out. You wouldn't believe what's in my head. I was so happy wasn't I? Remember when I used to drop in at the start when he went away, I was so happy wasn't I? I didn't care how slowly the time went. I wanted it slow, I didn't hide from it, I wanted the time to make myself ready.

I had the future then, all my love to make a future. It was just a kiss. Now everyday, I come and hide in here. I've nobody else to talk to. I haven't even told you about the limousine stopping for me the other day, whenever it was now. I can't keep track. I nearly got in Anna. This limousine stopped and they asked me to get in and I was on the verge of it, I swear. I'm so afraid. I dream of somebody touching me. Can you hear me Anna?

Have you talked to Donal?

Why would I talk to him? I won't even look at him. I want to make him suffer. He thinks you're an alcoholic whore did I ever tell you that? Martin didn't like it in here either. Martin said this place gave him the creeps, and you too. We argued about it a few times. You know Moore stood in the door one time and blocked him trying to get out? Nothing was said but Martin swore he would never set foot in the place again and he asked me not to either. He said I enjoyed the men gloating over me, drooling over me. He is so blind. Are they really all so blind Anna? I was bringing my love into the shop, I was brightening the place up wasn't I, with my love. Like you said. They were always glad to see me weren't they? Now what do they see me as? Proof that all their warnings are true, that it couldn't last, that nothing lasts.

I can't believe that Anna. I don't want to believe it. This limousine was out there in the street and I could have got in and been taken away and who would have bloody noticed? Nobody. Have you ever felt your hand going down between your own legs and you can't stop it. When I was a girl...

Anna pats her on the back of her hand. Everything'll work out. Have your cry. Donal's not a bad person. He was a lovely child, always helping people. He's troubled but he's not bad. The two of you seemed to get on well enough together didn't you?

He's a coward. I stood at his door the other night and told him what I thought of him. I said that he's going to have to throw me out on the street if he wants rid of me. I'm going to make his life fucken miserable. I think he told Martin out of spite, out of jealousy, to keep me away from his best friend. And now it's backfired on him. I'm so angry at him it's making me sick. I'm going to make him pay. Why won't he come back Anna? Why can't he see?

You have your cry sweetheart. It'll work out I promise you.

Like it did for you? Do you know what I've heard about you? It didn't work out for you.

Have your cry sweetheart.

Anna pours the tea into both their cups. There is a small chip out of the tip of the fat bird's neck spout. The splashing brown liquid is a drink of pure essence of loneliness. Anna fills three spoons with sugar stirs in the milk. She says

Maybe he'll come back. People have to find their own way. Some men are scared of what they want.

He better hurry Anna. I'm so greedy I've no strength left. My skin is on fire. I could take that hot spoon and rub it along my throat and I wouldn't be able to resist. Even to see it cloud over if I breathe on it. Can you hear me?

Dragging his boots across the lino, Moore comes down the hall.

She knows he is standing behind her, she can hear the way he breathes only through his nose like an animal

can hear his bones cracking. He is looking at her hair which she has in a loose plait, her strong bare shoulders and the skin of her back between the straps of her dress, the dress she bought with Martin, a geometric print on a silky material, a slight tuck at the waist. Growling at the little constellation of moles across her shoulder blades like a man who hates the stars, figuring out how he can reach there and conquer them

like an animal comes into the scullery and stands too close to her, resting his groin on the edge of the table near the little blue puckered jug. Veronica stirs her tea slowly, tinkling her lost sheep bell. The spoon turning in circles, the room, the world, clockwise, anticlockwise

Anna must have left the kitchen because it's just the two of them alone together. She wasn't paying attention. Nothing makes sense Veronica. People appear and don't appear.

Moore will be cleanly shaved, always scrubbed, trying to hide his smell which she knows is vinegar metallic under the cheap aftershave. His hair is parted in the middle like a farmer. Out of the corner of her eyes she can see his forearms and the thick pelt of black hair, the long fingers. He wears rings and a gold chain around his raw throat. It is all an expression of his authority, wherever he gets it from. He drops in every day to check on Anna, been doing that for years she's been told, keeping an eye on her and the men. He sometimes spends an hour in the shop with the watchers when he has nothing better to do. Once when she was passing the door along the street he accidentally swept a cloud of dust out of the shop against her. Right in front of her, he took the brush pole and angrily broke it over his thigh and threw the pieces far down the road.

Brushed and scoured, he stands his ground like the world is against him, like it might come up behind him, his boots squarely planted. She can imagine him lifting weights in a dingy bedroom or boxing in a shed. His face is swarthy, the small eyes far back under his forehead. His mouth is brutal and a bruised colour. He will have two red stars tattooed on his earlobes.

This is what she will see if she is able to look up at him, which sometimes she isn't because of the rude helpless greed for her in that stare of his. She finds that she keeps her eyes busy when she speaks to him, which she allows to happen as little as possible. Maybe it is his lust that makes him incomprehensible sometimes and vulgar. She is sure he is often imagining something else when he stands before her. Once she saw him showing the length of his tongue to the watchers. Saw him another time down the lane supporting himself with one hand against the wall while he took a piss, and she must have delayed a second because he looked round suddenly

he senses her anywhere near him smells her feels it

and caught her and she ran all the way back to the house.

He will be sifting her body for a crack, a flaw, a way in, like her skin is something he has never seen before, a delicacy that angers him, an insulting sweetness that can't be real until he has it in his hands, in his mouth. He is like a man who has witnessed something no one else believes in, and he is enraged.

Sit down Moore, for fuck's sake.

He does as he's told. The chair creaks under his weight.

Veronica plays with the spoon. Can't lift the cup to her lips either because she is afraid of where to put her eyes or how she will drink, if her lips make too much noise or her teeth scrape the rim the noise might make him explode.

She has to make light of it, try to be funny around him, sarcastic, mocking, cruel even.

Everything under control then Mr Moore? Nobody stepping out of line? Nobody asking for what they don't deserve?

Is that all you do, cry your eyes out these days? Heard about you and the fancy limo by the way... You...

What? I don't understand you sometimes.

Forget it.

What did you hear then?

In defiance now she takes a sip of tea, risks a glance at him. His eyes are moving all over her, through her hair, down her throat. He has her bent over the table, her dress pulled up over her hips, he's torn her knickers off and he's got a hold of her, and he won't put it in her until she begs him to, go on, beg me

A seagull cries somewhere above the shop and she laughs.

Crying over those two... toerags.

She gives him her best warning glare.

Two fucken stuck up deadbeats, he says firmly, and you know it. No fucken clue what to do with a woman... Wasters. Aren't I right? You... They couldn't... Two useless pricks.

You're the prick.

You want to see it?

Suddenly stands up and goes for his zip. You want to see it?

She knows there is no way to call his bluff. I thought you had a bit more decency than that, she tries, keeping her eyes lowered.

Decency? Whose decency? I know what you want, he says, leaning over the table now with his hands flat on the cover. Don't I? I can see inside…you know it. Right inside it… womb. I know what you need. Aren't I right?

She makes a face to show she thinks this is ridiculous, tiresome, keeping her eyes out of reach of his.

Eventually he sits down again. When he tries to remove his hands from the table, the plastic cover has stuck to his palms and everything is lifted and rattles and the tea spills into her saucer. She is glad of it, now she has something to do, putting the table to rights, tutting, hoping he feels clumsy.

Him going on talking and mumbling meanwhile: You're a snob, that's what I know about you. I know where you come out of don't forget… Now you're hanging… blue eyes and trying to get up the ladder. But underneath it all, you're wanting more… Crying your eyes out in here every day with an old woman. I know how to stop you crying. Just… give… word and I'll give you plenty to smile about. You wouldn't have to do a thing… close your eyes and leave it to me. You say gentle and I'll be gentle. You say hard and I'll break you in three. And I know you'll say hard. One try, that's all I'm asking. One… try and if it's not what you want, I'll leave you alone. Right alone… It's a fucken shame… woman like you lonely like…. you're lying in bed sweating at night. Madcap stuff. One try that's all I'm asking. I'll open you right up the way you want. And there I was last night thinking… window you know what I was thinking. Me and you were…

MARTIN PUT HIS HANDS behind his head and stretched arched his torso in front of her. He had sat her down on the edge of a stranger's bed and opened his zip stood there. After he had done circling her, she had not been sure what to do

what she wanted and he was aware of it.

brought her two hands up towards his groin and settled his balls on her palms.

drew her fingernails lightly up and down the length of him.

My cherry red nails along the swollen vein.

She wanted to kiss the tip, her lips did, they wanted to touch that tender blind animal but she couldn't.

She knew what to do and she couldn't. She closed one hand more tightly around his cock, deep down near the root where the pale hair

and began to pull and push back. I want to come on you and lick you clean, he said.

She knew what to do but she couldn't. What was that great grieving of a sea she was floating in

that sea she was pumping higher and wider with each thrust of her hand. She was frightened suddenly, suffocated

took her hand away angrily.

She slid across the bed and with her back to him returned her breasts to the coarse black net of her bra. The noise of his zip and his belt buckle shook tipped the room from side to side and she pressed herself down on the bed like a boat. Then he was sitting beside her, his arm around her.

Without a word he pulled her head down towards his

shoulder. Without a word. If he had spoken at all, she would have screamed at him. This man she had met downstairs at a dinner table and followed up to the bathroom. This man with his cheekbones and stiff casual cock that made her grieve for herself. Who made you cry with his cock in your hand. His slanting blue eyes and his fresh mouth. They would all know, they would be imagining what was going on up there, sneering at her sexual audacity.

They met again the next day. Went for a meal together. She took him home to her bed and very gently he lay on top of her and went inside her. He came with his mouth on hers and she held him knew it wasn't great for him. She turned away from him and wept again.

The next morning she made him breakfast. She was standing at the sink washing up when she felt him behind her.

I didn't hear your chair I was so lost in my dreams, didn't notice you had stopped talking. You kissed my neck while your hands pulled up my skirt over my hips. I was wearing tights, sheer black tights. I had a plate in my hand as I pushed back with my hips against you and leaned my elbows on the edge of the sink. I was wearing washing-up gloves and the suds dripped down my arms. I looked at my rings on the draining board like they were some other woman's. You peeled down my tights my knickers kissing the outside of my legs as they went down. I shivered at your breath against my ass. Then I felt your fingers go in between my legs and find me, open me, find me and I was wet and swollen almost immediately. Through the kitchen window I could see the street, and the trees which they had shorn the week before, the hacked away branches, bright yellow wounds and black branches and in front of that my reflection, and yours. It kept getting in the way; I didn't want to see our reflection, I wanted a big sky, a pack of gulls screaming but our reflection blocked the view. I didn't want to look at us or I couldn't. Then so quickly you had slipped inside me, your cock—you see, now I can use that word

now I love that word, then I had no word for you, or for me— your cock went into me like it was the easiest thing, like the mark of my truth. You put your hands on my bare hips and started to take me hard so hard like you were using me, like I could have been any woman, and I panicked. That grief sadness pain filled me up again. I pushed you away, dropping the plate on the floor and smashing it. Looking at you I didn't know you, I had no idea who you were although a moment ago I was telling myself how much I could love you,

got my tights up and ran to the bathroom and cried. Cried so deeply.

She pushed him off and ran into the bathroom and wept so deeply.

He called every day and each time she said she needed more time. She didn't understand what she was feeling. Finally she invited him round for dinner. He arrived soaked by the rain. She lit the fire. She drank. When he came near her and started to kiss, she told him to wait. Then she pulled the spare mattress in front of the fire and undressed down to her underwear, her favourite white vest with the rip and black lace knickers. She laid him down on his back and when she had made him hard with her hand and her mouth, she put him inside her. His long easy cock.

put his hands on her breasts and used her hips and knees to bring him deep inside and tighter and tighter until he came, both of them came together, and she was crying again

but the sadness was lighter he had been at the centre of her and the centre had burst open

be gentle with me. At least for a while and you can have everything.

THE CANDLES ARE MATING; first the fat white candle on the mantlepiece wriggles and bends and judders and then a few seconds later the long candle up on the dressing table tries to do exactly the same. Sitting on the bed against her pillows, she can see it all reflected in the long oval mirror her granny gave her. Wearing her big wool cardigan and knickers and nothing else. When she reaches for the wine bottle she finds it's finished already. She would normally be drunk. Thick red wine.

Gets up and goes to the bedroom window, the wood cold on the soles of her feet, the candles shaking in her wake. Darkness in the silent street, in every crack. The pavement is dry, the sky invisible. Lights like a string of pearls. Nobody on the dirty bench in its yellow greasy blur. Across the street she can see into the kitchen of the new people who have just moved in, a couple. They are in the kitchen. The window is open. The girl is wearing a short denim skirt and a red vest. She is beautiful, foreign, her lustrous brown skin makes everything look hard and crude and mean. She is cooking, talking over her shoulder. The lad gets up from the table lifts her hair and kisses the nape of her neck. She turns around to face him and with a single finger he pulls her vest away so he can look down admire her breasts

The foreign girl laughs.

Where are you how I laughed for you I wish I was that lad with her breasts to kiss all night

looks up towards the dirty bench again and Moore's sitting there now, his legs crossed swinging his leg, smoking.

She sees herself in the dark mirror and stops.

Once speeding down the motorway in his battered red van, with Martin driving, he put his hand between her legs and made her come, the white lights ahead and the swarms of red lights pouring toward her like she had once told him she dreamed about

the faces going by knowing nothing or maybe doing the same.

the number of times in the back of his red van

He surprised her at work in a suit and tie, met her outside the door and pretended to be some stranger smitten with her and could he buy her lunch and he touched her under the table with a fork, pressing the prongs into her thigh

how he loved her to suck him in the morning before she left for work, leaning across the bed in her coat, her bag on her shoulder, her mouth made up because he had once told her he liked that

my eyelashes fluttering against the tip of his cock

the time in the lane on the way home in the rain and his stained knees

the night she pretended to be his sister

him wearing her corset and makeup dancing against the wall with his shadow

He was tall and charmingly chaotic. He was always cheerful. She was seen as one more proof of how lucky he was. People wanted his company and the girls fell over themselves to be near him although he was often too busy talking or explaining to notice. Laying a floor, digging a garden, writing an article, a chat with so and so, a pint with somebody else, his language classes, helping some girls move a sofa, an hour alone with his guitar in the back of the van, a walk with Donal, some protest meeting in a hotel, a friend arriving in town, organising the lighting for a film shoot—every day of his had an ingenious inconsistent chronology that he was shy about admitting to or superstitious perhaps, he was very superstitious, his mother was an astrologer he was always saying, whenever Veronica would meet him in the evening, weary and somehow smudged after work and irritable and wanting only to go home and change her clothes and do nothing at all while he was making plans to meet somebody or catch this new band or have a look at some pub that was reopening after a renovation.

or she saw him in the shower and wanted to be the water pounding against his golden breastplate of hair the soap in his hands the towel on the floor like another woman anything but the woman who could never keep him and she couldn't tell him that.

Be my whore

Be my little boy

I want to hear your phantasies

Let me see you fuck your ex tell her how good it is now

Pretend you are dying pretend you are on your deathbed and I come in to give you your last time

Now she is standing alone in a mirror in a dark house and who will she be.

What are you going to do Veronica.

Who are you going to be Ronnie.

A NOISE PULLS HER OUT of the mirror and takes her running to the bedroom door. She listens. It must be Donal. Him sneaking in. Back into the house, his house. Wrapping the cardigan around her, she goes straight down the stairs. She doesn't know what she will say to him, she wants to see his face, to make him see her face, her eyes, make him see what he has done. But the rooms are empty, empty of people but not darkness, a different darkness behind each door. She turns on all the lights.

sits in the kitchen at the table with its thick bow legs. There's the bowl of pretty flower seed packets. The table surface marked with dents and rings and burns Donal in his sick moods calls the constellation of the damned and drops a grape or flicks his ash on the tortured worlds. Silver candlesticks like faces nose to nose she has polished again and again and buys the candles for from the woman who sits on the deck chair in the porch of the cathedral. Another bowl of fruit going bad. She tells herself she should eat. It's been two days, maybe more. She begins to roll a joint for herself from his stash. One thing she learned to do in this house is roll a good joint. People used to ask for her hands especially at the parties, all the times he brought people back late at night. A party almost every weekend, spontaneous, loud, drunken, and she would come down from her room and join in.

The tap drips into the foamed up sink she goes to turn it off. She was washing up and must have stopped to do something else. What was it distracted her. The heavy black wrought iron frying pan with the singed wooden handle. Hadn't she made up her mind not to do any cleaning up of the mess. The whole house could rot for all she cared. She checks the water with her finger and it is still warm.

When had she been doing the dishes.

She can't remember runs back upstairs to her bedroom where one of the candles has gone out. At the window she looks for Moore on the dirty bench. He's gone. So are the couple across the street—the girl lies moaning with a mouth at her brown nipple. Each house along the street with its lighted windows and dark windows is like a person, with different scenes going on in the various rooms at the very same time, some of the rooms unused blocked up or just spare and forgotten. If she were a house now there would be a hundred rooms blazing with light and nobody in them. Echoes of ghosts laughing down the hallways with mosaic floors. No front door, the walls crumbling, a huge overgrown garden and clothes hanging in the branches.

Or a cottage by the sea with its roof caved in.

To turn around now and face the emptiness of this room. Just herself among the furniture. Like a witch she hovers over the cauldron of her jewels. The padded ivory white box like the cover of a wedding album, lined with treacherous purple inside.

The locket he bought her, the feather earrings, the scarlet glass snake with the black tongue for around her wrist. Rings necklaces bangles the silver torc the white choker rub them and the days reappear, the other faces moods the other selves will it never stop all this changing

We are always changing and we are trapped

My aching wisp of a body trapped inside the hard world.

She lights the joint again spits on the oval mirror. The phone is ringing.

It won't be you.

A scar of spittle on the glass. And the few loose pearls like little eggs she found in the zigzag lane.

But what about those times in her palace bed, the nights she had gone to bed to think about Martin, to think about him in the way she thought was best, to summon him to her, lying on her back her legs open, touching herself, for there was often a phantasy she slipped into, one of many

the three of them lying sleeping in a big bed, and Martin would quietly roll on top of her go inside her and fuck her very softly and Donal was asleep on the other side of the bed, maybe asleep, maybe half awake, and it turned her on, the closeness of the three of them, what about thoughts like that, had she been wrong to let herself have those thoughts. Martin had always told her to think about whatever she wanted... he said it was ok.

You said it was ok not to hide anything all the true beauty

WHEN THE FRONT DOOR OPENS a few hours later, she is sitting in the same position on the bed. She feels her heart has slowed to the slightest pulse, barely enough to push the blood through her veins. Her eyelashes and cheeks are wet; she must have been crying. The door shuts loudly, shaking the house. This time she doesn't move from the bed. He must be standing there, listening for her. Eventually, he makes up his mind and goes down the hall to the kitchen, his shoes on the wood, that noise that surrounds him of jewellery, of the creaking of leather in his belt, the coins in his pocket, the lips chewing, sticking, snorting—a noisy man, a banger and curser and thumper. He's probably drunk.

Veronica waits.

He could be so charming and so cruel. The first weeks there in the house, she had to fight against his attentiveness. Almost every night she was forced to go out with him or he would be continually knocking on her door to check on her. Or sit downstairs smoking with him while he went on and on about things she knew nothing about and didn't want to either. It got so bad she had to have a talk with him about it. She cooked a meal for the two of them, a shepherd's pie, which she knew he liked and told him straight that he was trying too hard, that she needed her space. It turned out to be a lovely evening; he seemed to relax completely for the first time and open up about himself, his father's death when he was a child, his mother and the men she went through, her restlessness and how it affected his own relationships with women, particularly the woman he had been engaged to. Yes, he had asked a woman to marry him. Without believing him, Veronica laughed to hear how he had proposed, in bed in the middle of the night, trying to wake her up after he had a dream he was at a wedding and she was marrying another man. He didn't know where she was now. He had treated her very badly he admitted and fell into one of his silences, rolling joint after joint, drinking glass after glass of whiskey. Only the following night, she heard him come back late, and he had brought people with him. Music went on. She could hear every word from the kitchen through the old floorboards. How many hours had she spent listening to those endless ridiculous earnest conversations they had, the furious arguments, the stories that were forgotten before they were told. She gave in tried on some different clothes in front of the mirror and went down to them. It was mostly men, and one very drunk woman. One of the men, an older man with a greying beard, wouldn't leave her alone. Older men were always attracted to her. This one spluttered the usual dross and put his hand on her knee under the table. When she looked at Donal for help the wickedness in his sly grin appalled her. She went back to bed. The man knocked at her door, pleading, then insulting and she had to sit with her back to it to stop him coming in. The next morning, in a rage, she had a go at Donal for not defending her but he claimed he couldn't remember any of it. Again, she thought it was another test. The bearded man was never seen again however. Some nights when she didn't go down to join them Donal might knock on her door or what was worse he went by laughing falsely to the toilet. He could have a horrible laugh. Then there were the girls he brought up into his bed. They were usually gone in the morning. One of them came into her room one night.

He is coming up the stairs. Step by step heavily. His hands brushing the walls and holding on to the banister. Outside her door, the commotion ceases abruptly. Is he trying to control himself or is he listening. He's probably blind drunk, swaying, full of rudeness. She has to decide whether to give him a sign that she's still awake.

Show me your courage, knock on my door and be a man.

But he goes into his room, slamming the door against her. He's fighting her. I am angry too, he's saying.

THE CAR DOOR SWINGS OPEN like a lover's arm in a bed.
   She sees a pair of black boots, sharply pointed.
   The trousers have embroidered cuffs.
   His knuckles, the hairless underside of his wrist.
   There are flowers on the leather seat, roses.
   Snowdrops. Autumn wildflowers.
   Smoke turns in the air, loosening curls.
   A black hat with a silk band.
   The shaved back of his neck.
   Knuckles stroked against her lips.
   Don't say a word. Let me dream.
   A single petal on the carpet.
   His shirt unbuttoned. His thick earlobe. His nostrils.
   The most miserly man wouldn't deny me this illusion.
   Please don't speak.

THE MORNINGS ARE THE WORST. The house is always older, as though she has been asleep for a long long time. Her hair is limp and dry. Although she tells herself it is pointless, and even tragic, she finds herself growing excited about what she should wear that morning, often trying on different knickers and tops in front of the oval mirror in its black wood. She hurries downstairs. First she stops at the door of the living room, because that would be where he would wait, on one of the sofas, reading a book. When she doesn't find him there she heads for the kitchen. She has stacked all the dirty plates from the party by the side of the sink but even the sight of them, and the mess of newspapers and cups and ashtrays on the big table isn't the end of her hope. He wouldn't come back and start cleaning up. Her heart won't surrender so easily. She checks in the garden where he might have chosen to sit until she woke, if the weather is fine, amused by all the rubbish lying around in the grass, on one of her blue chairs, to match his eyes. He isn't there either. She will make herself some tea, a pot of tea, and set out two cups and wait on the chair by the back door. Her hands will be trembling. She'll look at the sky and try to work out if it is a sky that heralds a great reunion, or if the trees are an ominous colour of green or if the gulls are high or patrolling the roofs. Even the rubbish she refuses to clean up can seem a perfect backdrop for his smile, his eyes that have flooded helplessly with his need for her and brought him back, for a kiss that will mean the silencing of this useless pain. Her nipples harden—two spears in the ground,

Martin said once. Is this the day, is everything ready, is this how the day will look.

Am I ready at last.

Slowly, against her will, the ache begins to grow again. Up from a wincing rippling distress in her heart, her throat goes dry, then a buttery taste in her mouth and her lips drain and cool— her lips get so cold. The trees whisper to each other that they're fed up, that this is not the day. Mocking, scoffing, the gulls head out towards the docks and the sea. The world takes a sip of her pain and turns its nose up. Maybe it wasn't enough, she didn't suffer enough. Maybe she's as selfish in her pain as she is greedy in her love. She should have stayed up later, ached more. She should have been less vain. She shouldn't have loved him so much. She shouldn't have told him the dreams in her mind. It was bad of her not to resist her fingers wanting to feel how wet she was.

I am so wet these days.

Each night when the limousine stops, she should honour her pain, hold her head high, and walk away.

She listens to the cars on the street leaving for work, the children on their way to school. These mornings she has to turn a light on in the kitchen, the one with the blue shade and golden tassels. The floor is growing cold, she can feel it around her ankles. She has to fill the kettle over a dirty sink, bad luck her granny always said.

Donal will be up in his room. He stays up through the night. She has decided to avoid him. It's nearly a week and they haven't spoken. He stays in bed all day, waiting for her to turn out her light. She should learn to sleep with the light on.

She will get dressed again and to escape the house, go up the street and under the tree to Anna's. She will sit in the kitchen with Anna stirring her tea or she might fry some bacon for sandwiches for the men and stand to talk with them around the doorway, throwing back her head proudly if one of the neighbours goes by and sees her there. The men ask about her sometimes, where she was born and bred but it is more to get the talk going than from any real curiosity. They fear sickness and death less than their own memories. They believe in laughter over truth. Then there will be the stories that fail to reach their end, that stop suddenly or turn into another story entirely, and she will almost understand how that is the very point of what they're trying to say.

Today the talk is about Gretta. She is one of the few women who hang about the shop. It's common knowledge she is in love with Moore, obsessed by him, McGrory says and taps the side of his head. Gretta has a little boy she calls Aaron and the social services have taken him away from her again. She was arrested recently for breaking the window of a police car. She gets drunk and turns up at the shop in a foul temper demanding to know where Moore is. She can be violent. Veronica saw the two of them by the garage door; Gretta was on her knees with her face in Moore's groin, sucking blindly extracting some pain out of him while he was fallen against the wall his hand raised at the moon, the fine curve of the moon and gripping her badly dyed blonde hair.

With Anna's shopping list, she will eventually walk the short distance to the indoor market. The men in overalls stare at her; she is their wives, their daughters, all the girls they've whispered to, their mothers, the women who have seen them cry. She is the days when their shoulders ached for the weight of the future, the nights when they laid their heads on a woman's breast and promised her whatever she wanted.

They catch each other's eyes and nod towards her as though they're saying, you see that, all we used to believe in, the softness of their skin, the gentle hands, their mad beliefs, the promises

wouldn't you like to teach her a lesson

They have seen her happiness, her long wait, the dreams widening her eyes, and now they see her abandoned. She looks deep into each face for one who is not glad to see her brought down.

Some of them don't talk to her anymore. They turn away from her, pretend to be busy, avoid her eyes.

In the indoor market, under the low black girders, she walks down the avenues of vegetable and fruit stalls, of boxes of unwashed carrots with their green plumes, bronzed onions, glossy soft tomatoes, parsley, fools' crowns of cabbages, white garlic, wine aubergines, celery, lacquered red chillies, turnip heads, passion fruits like bulls' testicles, clementines, seashell peaches and the dung piles of potatoes.

in a jacket and long scarf, or an ankle-length coat, she brings the heels of her boots down loudly on the flagstones. Pigeons flap between the girders blinking and still don't remember, and the fierce-eyed gulls open their wings and show their soft white armpits.

the forklifts glide backwards between the lorries.

behind her she pulls Anna's old tartan shopping basket with the damaged left wheel that only skids along. The fish man's bucket is up to the brim with heads and guts. She buys the vegetables for the soup Anna makes every lunchtime now that the cold days are here.

The men wink at each other.

Anna said to her, He'll be back if he loves you. He'll find himself outside your door whether he likes it or not.

And, You have yourself some fun in the meantime. He won't let you out of his sight when he comes back. He'll be getting under your feet.

And, Some dreams just aren't any good. Like some of the stories they try to tell you out there at the door. Doesn't matter how you tell them.

And, Wait till your arse is as big as mine.

One morning, she buys a tea from a girl in the tiny café, carries it out, sits on an empty crate, using the trolley as a table. She stirs with a plastic spoon watching the mists from the men's mouths like smoke signals. The tea is weak and hot against her lips. Rain drums on the roof of the market, dripping down across the big doorways. A yellow plum, a broken apple, a black streaked banana. What is thrown away. He is not coming back. She will never sit like this, sipping tea in a damp coat, thinking of the sounds he made that morning in bed, or the feel of his skin, or his ass when he's getting into his trousers, or what she will cook for him that evening. He is not coming back. How can she ever start all over again. Who says you have to start again. Why can't she say, No bloody more.

That's enough. I can't do it all again.

I am so alone I could not stop myself if one of those men came forward and simply offered me his hand. The earth gives us this food to carry on.

The day is in front of her with its painful truths buried in boxes of fruit and the eyes of old drunks

the truth in the steamed-up window of a café and the rain on a stack of potato sacks

and in the scald of the tea against her lips.

the forklift driver moves backwards towards the lorry with a load of banana boxes, a small radio taped to the metal,

music, she has forgotten about music, that there are songs.

One morning like this she noticed a young man, a boy, eating an orange tearing the fruit away from the skin with his teeth. He had his hood up, a fur trimmed hood. His hands were shaking.

He is not coming back.

You are not coming back.

I hate these colours, these shapes and colours, the smells, my damp overcoat with the fur collar, the sound of the rain—I never thought this would happen to me. I hate the poetry everywhere. I want a man to take me without poetry. I want his eyes to laugh at me when I look for poetry in his hands. I want his mouth to curse me when I kiss the burning tendon that links his weakness and his hunger.

Trick me.

Trick me into your bed.

Laugh in my face as I lie beneath you, wanting more.

THE BOY CAN'T BE MORE THAN SIXTEEN. Veronica offers him a cup of tea. He shrugs. She brings him a cup of tea and a sausage sandwich, watches him eat, his thin frantic red mouth. She likes the shape of his chin, white and gentle like a girl's, in the shadow of his hood. His eyes won't look at her. She sits with him in silence and watches the market.

Moore comes in the far door with another man, sees her immediately, smells her through all the scents of fruits and rain and rot and grease and lorry fumes, hears her breathing, her heart, sniffs her.

He would be a jealous man. A woman is his possession. All men are his enemies when he is with her. Gretta comes looking for him and they go off together and she is glowing happy when she returns, ready to go back and look after her child. Though sometimes Moore rejects her and she can be seen in the local bar, drinking, starting fights among the men. Veronica found her once outside on the street sitting on the curb and took her back to the house to sleep it off. Gretta fought and cursed; she wanted to sleep in the gutter, it's all I'm worth, I'm fucken worthless. She was gone in the morning and has never said a word about it.

So what are you doing today? You in school? What would you do today if you could do anything?

The boy says nothing to her questions. She notices him stiffen and look nervously about the place. Moore is approaching, striding down between the stalls, taking the greetings of the men as though he has a right to them. He wears a leather jacket she hasn't seen before, trainers and jeans on his long powerful legs. He is untouched by the rain. Veronica tells the boy to sit where he is and takes his hand. It is cold and thin. He pulls it free again.

Moore tells the boy to get lost and he does, running out into the rain. Before she can stop him.

Bully.

Moore says he's a thief. He's a druggie. A waster.

Veronica makes a face and stands up and gets ready to go.

He says she's not looking her best and offers to buy her a cup of tea. Says he knocked for her the other night.

Did you now?

Says, I thought you might be lonely. Maybe you were having a bath and wanted somebody to scrub your back. What... bingo. Hot...

He is childish and crude. He looks down the buttons on her coat as though he is tearing them off one by one. His eyes are grey and brown like a puddle.

Maybe I was having a bath, she says, tipping her face at him.

Let me guess. Candles and a glass of wine?

You'll never know will you? Never in a million years.

His face sours. Says, You're wasting yourself away on nothing. All I'm asking for is one chance. I know you, don't forget. I know what you're made of.

Crap. He talks hard man's crap.

I'm not Gretta, she tells him, you can't boss me about.

He moves right into her then, almost touching her. She turns her head away.

I want to have you, he says. You just have to say the word. One chance... One... That walk of yours, it's like I know what it means... like it is talking to me. I can hear you. I know the right way into you. And I know you'll… me afterwards. But I'll take it. And I'll wait till you ask me back. Whenever you want Veronica. Day or night. You're lonely. You're making yourself lonely. Aren't I right? I want to see you lying down with that hair spread out like you're falling.

My hair was touching his face.

like it was crawling away from me reaching out

for anything.

Look what is happening to me my love.

or I will ache so much I will forget.

DONAL IS CHANTING BEATING his skin drum beyond the wall. Monotonously like he is calling to something, coaxing, or he is taunting that he is the stronger. Her bottles tremble and tinkle on the bathroom shelf. She has to be stronger than him. She walks around half naked to show the drum that it has no power over a woman like her, it is a whinging self-pitying little boy that's all.

One kiss from me one true kiss would destroy you and all your big words and druggie drum and give your mystic a hard on

you didn't know existed here or in any world.

One drop of my piss would burn a hole in you

Sitting on the toilet, she peers at her own dim reflection in the black floor tiles, so far down, floating frightened between her knees

Who are you

You don't look like me

And suddenly she sees another room, a smoky room, and there are men talking. What is that blue armchair and the corner of that unmade bed. Whose are they. A single yellow flower like a lily in a cracked earthenware pot in a strange bath. Men waiting in an unfamiliar room just out of sight. These thoughts in her head come out of nowhere.

and as she glances down between her thighs she catches sight of something disgusting in the water below like some creature or spider in the bowl. She screams

runs into the hall.

Donal?

Barechested, drowsily, he comes to his door.

It's dead. There's a dead thing in the toilet, she tells him, straightening her skirt to keep from grabbing hold of him. He struggles not to look at her chest for she is wearing only a bra, her black bra with the tiny pink roses.

Hair, he says, when he comes out of the bathroom. And he carrries on past her into the room shutting the door quietly.

Her hair in the toilet bowl, the loose clumps of hair she had pulled out of her brush and dropped into the toilet. She goes into her room. It is bleak in there and tasteless. The room of a woman who refuses to accept she has lost. A cat is walking along the dirty bench. The night before

very late some night recently she saw a fox around the bench and ran down to the door and into the street

she was sure she had seen it

the rubbish bags were out for collection

Terribly restless, she goes down to the kitchen. The drumming has stopped at least. The kitchen table sink window door garden the house—everything is part of her, it's all stuck to her and what she needs is to feel what isn't her

free of her.

No me. How is she going to get through the evening. Suddenly it seems impossible, beyond her. She is going to break.

Oh my god

She only ever brushes her hair before washing it and she didn't wash her hair tonight.

hears laughter upstairs. A woman's laugh. The bastard has sneaked some girl in. He's been drumming for some young one. While she is about to crack up he brings some girl up to his room to tickle her. Laughter smothered, suppressed. She runs up the stairs and kicks his door.

Look at what you've done and you're in there with some slaps his face.

How could she make him understand what he had done.

61

How could he pretend to just carry on when she was in so much pain. Had he ever felt this kind of pain. I told you about myself, that I had been making myself ready, that it had to be everything or I wouldn't be interested. Did you hate that in me want to destroy it. He stands there staring at me like he has heard this before, that he doesn't really believe me. This is your fault. Will I go from house to house, banging on doors for the rest of my days. Let me in, somebody let me in. There are women who keep their life a secret, who take every happy moment like a jewel and store it away like treasure. When they're left alone they slide out the golden tabernacle chest and arrange the pieces on their scented beds. At least I have these memories to keep me warm, they say. But me, if I am left alone now, then I have nothing and there has always been nothing. I get cold. I get so cold. Why won't he help me.

Why won't you help me? she says to him, disgusted at herself.

I didn't think you wanted me to.

This is your fault. Isn't it? Say this is your fault for a start. Apologise for a start.

I'm sorry. I told you I was sorry.

When? And who have you got in there?

He acts confused.

I don't care who anyway. Don't believe a word he says, she calls over his shoulder.

What are you talking about Veronica? I'm sorry. I'm telling you now again. I'm sorry, and his hand comes out towards her

his bare arm her bare arm his bare shoulders his chest her

Leave me alone. She turns into her room slams the door. Her precious sensual bed and its patterned duvet and pillows is vulgar chic so shallow so shallow Veronica who were you kidding

pulls down her suitcases from the top of the cupboard.

SHE CAME IN OFF THE MISTY COURTYARD through a door with a glowing red fanlight. The man in the black uniform was sitting behind a desk studying a bank of monitors which showed the different rooms. She knew her way; she took the blue steps to the long stone corridor. Deep in the walls the small barred windows were iced over. Her footsteps went echoing on before her. At the door of the old shed, she knocked, worried her hand would stick to the rusty latch. The men were sitting in a circle on the cold floor. At the centre of their circle was an enormous wooden bowl and each of them had a hand held out over the bowl and from their wrists the blood dripped into the bowl.

They spread a ragged piece of soft white fur on the floor for her to stand on.

SHE SLEEPS AND WAKES and sleeps again, moves from room to room, chair to chair, in search of that ideal position, the perfect light in the window, the humid smell from the fireplace, the sound of the day's routines outside, for her skin to be the right temperature, the angle of the armchair towards the back door

from which she can see what to do, what her next move should be, and how she got here in the first place. What happened Veronica. Is this the crime of one kiss. She has never looked back on her life before; she has never thought her life was a story, or that it should be. There was the relationship with Phil, the relationship with Kieran, the long lonely wait for her big love, and then Martin. None of the other details mattered. And as she wanders about in the house day and night, she never doubts it still, love is her breath,

she would never doubt it she says aloud horrified by the friendlessness of her own voice echoing in the kitchen,

never, never, she would shout at the mirror, or in the back garden, I would rather die.

I don't want this to be a story. Just another story.

I am not a story.

I would rather forget you.

I would rather die.

I am so horny my love.

Is this the true test of my love.

YOU ARE IN THE LIMO, being driven through the streets at night. The rain is pouring down

it's a summer evening the entire city is out on the streets and the moon is a giant shell of pearl. This man is beside you.

You are completely naked. Except for a long heavy necklace looping down across your belly. A thick silver locket cold on your belly just above the line of your hair. The street lights splash across your body.

The car smells of

In the window the man's face is reflected as he watches the people dancing on the pavements. His calm austere face. He has seen it all before. He knows too well the people will go home dissatisfied. The car has to move slowly.

In the mirror, you catch the eyes of the driver on your body. Your breasts so soft free more buoyant and full than you've ever seen them before.

Your long nipples.

The stiff folds of his ears.

reach out your hand for his crotch. You can't wait anymore.

IN THE LATE NIGHT SHOP, where she is choosing a bottle of wine, Moore comes up beside her.

Drinking alone again are you eh? He reeks of a cheap aftershave. She flaps her hand under her nose. He is wearing a white short-sleeved shirt and black belt in his pressed jeans. A teenager's dress sense. His eyes look her brazenly up and down, from her boots and ragged jeans and up across her hips to her breasts loose in the yellow T-shirt she took from Martin, under an old knitted black shawl she wears in some moods, up to her throat and her ears and her hair tied back. Then he places himself by her shoulder and studies the bottles.

She folds her arms through the crooked handles of the shopping basket.

Who says I'm going to drink it alone?

… and teabags and a lettuce, he says with a nod to the basket. Hardly a meal fit for a queen is it? Red or white so? The thing to do…

Maybe saying something about the age of the wine, a good year, he reaches for a bottle. She finds herself watching the way it lies in his hand, the fingers closed around the glass curve.

She hears him mention Donal's name and has to ask him to repeat what he said.

… that Donal character getting into a cab and… you not dressed… for a night on the town… bollix.

He puts the bottle back, selects another, and holds it in front of her so that the base of the bottle is touching her breasts.

Try this one.

All she can think is that Donal has gone out again and she will be alone in that house for another night and how many nights before he stumbles in again.

Try this one. Trust me. I know a thing or two about a good grape.

So do you want a glass? she says as sour as she can make it sound. She takes hold of the bottle by the neck to avoid his fingers. The label is a lonely purple.

He looks her in the eye, it would be a long look but she turns away quickly to keep it casual and surveys the wine bottles again.

His breath against her neck, catching in her hair, the steak he's eaten.

Another time, he says, and there would be a wry smile goes with it, but she doesn't look and he leaves her there seething in her shawl under the eye of the security camera.

UNDER THE STARS SHE SITS on an old deck chair in the garden to drink her wine. The stars in clusters and shapes and signs that Martin was good at. The zodiac. I am blind to my own fate.

and cold but can't bear the thought of moving, of standing up and moving her limbs, the loneliness it makes her feel, the vast empty air around her. And she smelled perfume in the house not like her own and she hasn't worn it recently anyway because she's out totally dry and can't afford to buy more. She has no money left and she's living in the house of the man who destroyed her love, sitting in his garden under the stars that somebody else is probably doing a better job of looking at and being wise about than her.

I am a statue in a city of love

The wine tastes of soil and berries. Gently, the wind shakes the bushes like those prayer wheels he told her about that you spin to bless your journey. Even the wind is afraid of what lies ahead.

light from the kitchen in a big oblong and a smaller square on the grass and the paper plates and cups shrinking deflating slowly like balloons mushrooms shrivelling up leaves even her breasts are smaller he used to make them grow with his attention

What are you going to do Veronica.

She picks a crumb of cork from the tip of her tongue and her heart gets an ache. Her nails against her tongue. Every touch leaves her bereft.

What are you going to do Veronica.

 Two voices reach her from the next garden, from behind the bush and the woven fence. Two lads. City accents. She is happy to listen to them. She hears that one of them has bought a new car. That they were out separately the night before at different clubs. That one of them got drunk and one talked a phone number out of a girl with long red hair and green eyes. They open cans of beer and smoke grass one says is the best in ages. She can smell it. She wants to get so stoned she can't move. To sit and flirt with two strange lads in the back garden and let them make her laugh. She considers calling out hello to see what would happen, she has almost convinced herself to be brave when one of them mentions Donal's name. In a quieter hushed voice one tells the story that he had been at a party the week before where Donal had gone crazy. Threw furniture around, attacked people, screaming, waving a frying pan, and they had to drag him out. Veronica has to stop herself from demanding to hear more because the subject quickly changes to a girl by the name of Miranda who was seen walking down the street that same day, back from wherever. Each of them it is quickly clear has spent a night with this girl Miranda and has yet to forget it. Veronica listens as they describe at length how she kissed, the unnatural power of her tongue, her teeth, the words they thought she was saying in her kisses, the mad urging shocking words they thought they could hear, how she arched her back when they were at her breasts, her sighs and groans that frightened them, the fear in her own eyes for herself as she pulled them on top of her—they each agreed it was the animal erection they had always dreamed of. Touching their cans together, they raise a toast to her. Veronica has already slipped her hands into her jeans, in under her knickers and glides a finger down and up lightly in the moist warm richness treasured under her lips, up and down lightly, wetter and wetter. She needs them to carry on talking. Anything would do, just their voices would be enough

and the crowd of panting spying stars through her half closed eyes.

she gasps too loudly

I HAVEN'T COME TO FIGHT. And I'm positive there's another woman in this house, a woman with grey cobwebby hair that covers her shoulders. Every time I go into a room I expect to see her. I've heard her laughing. See what's happening to me. I don't want to fight Donal. I need to talk to you. There's an enormous pink full moon tonight. They're all out at the dirty bench, the men and the local youngsters. I had half a mind to go out and sit down among them, and listen. Anything but another night in that room.

She knocks.

Donal is on the floor, his ankles crossed like a kiss in front of his groin, his bare torso resting against the bottom of the bed. She can tell immediately he is in one of his gloomy pits from the way his profile sags. He is like a dancer resting after a passionate scene. The smell of a candle recently died reminds her of so many of her own nights alone. He glances at her briefly, then bows his head waiting on his punishment, her wrath. It is the trick of weakness. He hasn't shaven in a few days either.

his final night and she is the priest come to hear his last confession. The priest she seduced, tied to a chair and robbed of his garments. The sanctified cloth rubs against her breasts, the prison air creeps up between her thighs...

You called sir, she says, trying to be light. Don't worry, I haven't come to fight.

Without waiting to be invited, she takes the bottom cushion from the chair drops it on the floor. She sits down at an angle to him, stroking her big smooth moon knees. He keeps his head bowed, contemplating the cross of his legs, the cat's cradle.

Just let me sit here. I am seeking comfort in the company of the man who has ruined me, that's why I'm crying, that's all. For myself. I don't know whether you can hear me.

He moves his head, maybe just stretching his neck, but maybe to show he did hear her. She can't tell anymore what is said and what isn't.

What is and what isn't. Who is and who isn't. All those questions I used to ask you—remember? Because I wanted to know, I tried my best to want to know. And to annoy you also. Remember the butterfly? I was out in the park and a butterfly, a big green and pink butterfly flew into my mouth. The day before you had been talking about something, your magic or something, and words, about your name, having to search in different countries to find your magic name to be able to begin. Start your journey you said. But you wouldn't tell me what it was, your magic name. Or maybe it was something entirely different. Some other nonsense. A butterfly flew into my mouth and I had to pick it off my tongue and it was injured and I knew I had to save it. So I ran back here and all I could think about was showing you or getting your help, Donal will know what to do and what it all means. Remember? I was so upset. I was hysterical. And I was screaming at you not to let it die. And what did it mean. You were doing everything you could. And then when it died I was so scared and I hit you didn't I? And I didn't want to know how you got rid of it. What does it mean Donal what does it mean Donal? You were so good with me. I wouldn't leave the house for days. You were so sweet to me.

He reaches out his hand toward her. His eyes with their wet skin are all concern and compassion. The muscles stand out on the pale inside of his lower arms. His silver ringed fingers are thick and hooked, the nails are slightly too long. She can smell his sweat, from the matted brown hair in his armpits. His belly sags slightly. The weak hollow of his chest. The palm is a shock of fine red broken lines, smashed. A sign of what. The money line, the heart line, the life line all smashed.

you will travel, and learn nothing. You will kiss and you won't see.

He says, This is not what I wanted either Veronica.

Veronica. Who she.

Scratching his beard, he says, I feel terrible about what's happened, really terrible. It's a mess.

Donal, remember the day you me and Josie were out all day together. We went in for one drink at lunchtime and we were there till closing. I liked Josie. She had youth and ease and she was so pretty. She was in love with you and you had no idea. Or you hated her for it. I remember watching the two of you that day. The way she looked at you and how it could make you embarrassed and you'd forget what you were saying. She made you blush. She ran her hands through your hair. She leaned over and kissed you. I could see it in her eyes. We talked about Martin who she had never met. I wanted to feel the way she did, I wanted to have that warmth in my skin. The whole bar admired her. She could have asked for anything and they would have given it to her gladly. I saw a good side to you that day. You restrained yourself, she was charming you. And then what happened later. What happened later while I was lying in my bed trying to sleep and missing Martin so badly. She came into my room and got into bed beside me. She was soaked with sweat. I could smell the sex from her. And she had been crying. I held on to her. I asked her what was wrong and she put a finger on my lips and I could smell what had to be you on her finger. She slid down between my legs and I let her. I let her, even though she was still probably crying, her face right between my legs. I lay there and it was delicious and I just knew you had sent her in to me, I knew it and she loved you so much she had done it. I thought of the two of us as cruel and vicious and I lay there and pushed her face harder into me. And I thought that's what we're like, that's what we share, Donal and me. And we said nothing about it. And you got rid of Josie soon after like you got rid of all of them. Remember all this. Or am I making it all up or

there's the front door, the heavy brass knocker. Neither of them move. His face is angry now. He stares across her at the fireplace, at the odd candlesticks, silver and brass. Around his neck, he wears a thin strand of leather. He has a silver ring on his right thumb with an engraving of what looks like little black spiders, or stars. His feet are a good shape, little tufts of hair on his toes. She has never really thought about him before as a body. It was always just his mournful eyes and his mouth, the flow of words from his mouth, his posh jigsaw accent.

We used to talk all night. I was so honest with you. I thought I was learning from you. Thought you were helping me wait, helping me get ready for him to come back so that I was perfect for him.

Why did you tell him? I've been trying to understand. Is it about honesty? You said I wouldn't have told him so you had to. Maybe I would have forgotten it even happened. I already had. Maybe it was between you and me. I thought we understood each other. I am angry at the both of you, him for believing you.

For being so weak. For running away at the first sign of trouble. You know him, is he really so weak? Was I so wrong about him? How could he let it all go over one moment? Unless he wanted to be free of me anyway. Unless he was looking for a way. I hate these crumbling endless words. Now you sit there in your gloom robbing me of my pain.

Why did you tell him Donal? Do you hear me?

The knocker shakes the house again. It will be Moore.

He says, glaring at her fiercely, You were daring me to. You were daring me to tell him. You wanted me to tell him. You were taking revenge on him that's what I thought. You wanted him to see that he couldn't just leave you alone whenever he felt like it. You wanted to do something to show him and you chose me. You used me to tell him. Revenge for something or other. Or you were the one afraid. You don't even know it do you? I'm the fool here.

I KISSED YOU AND YOU LEARNED NOTHING from it. I kissed you and you wouldn't listen. You heard what you wanted to hear. I kissed you for joy and you twisted it into an ugly thing. I kissed you and it should have disappeared in an instant, a beautiful frail thing to hold up to the light but you caught it and pinned it down and wanted to show it off. You couldn't keep it between me and you. Your pain is fake. You're the counterfeit, the thing you've always accused everybody else of. You're your own nightmare now and I hope it scares you to death.

For her birthday Martin took her to the opera. It would be her first time. She was thirty years old. The long black dress she bought herself had a very low neck and was gathered at the back into a large bow. By sheer chance, she had found a pair of old-fashioned ivy green pointed heels to go with it and couldn't resist although they were very expensive. The dress showed off her shoulders and arms and made the most of her bust. He was wearing a dove grey linen suit when she met him in the theatre bar, and a red tie. She wanted to kiss him on behalf of every woman in the world. People stared at them, she thought, noticed how beautiful they were together. One man lifted his cocktail to her honour when she finally allowed him to catch her eye. They drank champagne from some gorgeous flower-shaped flutes but decided they wouldn't steal them because they were going to play at being people who did this all the time, who were accustomed to luxury and being pampered, a couple on their first formal date, they decided.

You have to seduce me, she told him. All I need is a fan.

Made from the bones of nightingales, he said.

Seduce me.

They had seats on the balcony to the side of the stage. The chairs were covered in lustrous red velvet. Gas lamps in copper cases burned along the walls and between the decorated pillars huge chandeliers of glass dangled their exquisite timeless teardrops. Below her, over the edge of the balcony, the women were excited by their own bodies, their bare arms and necks, their hair and naked human eyes. The men were covered up. There was no need for names or words or explanations. Words were little jewels and brooches and cufflinks. Her own body was part of this great mass of perfumed flesh. She loved the way the men were clearly men and the women had their own part to play. The extravagant length, the weight of those magnificent brocaded curtains suspended in the great arch—it had to conceal a place where only passion was real.

a delicate mirage place that can only be revealed in a certain false light the way some old paintings can only be shown after the sun has gone down.

She told him she was the happiest woman alive.

Then the orchestra, the polished wood and brass and the black suits, and a woman appeared on the stage

a woman in a torn and bloodied peasant's frock with her big powdered breasts almost bared and began to sing.

At first, Veronica was so turned on she could hardly sit still. She wanted to get down on her knees and suck him there and then but whenever she let her hands wander along his thigh he seemed too engrossed in the performance, and patted the back of her hand. There was a scene where the heroine was kneeling and gripping her bodice with both hands like she wanted to rip it off and the men gathered in a circle around her were shocked by her tragedy, outraged

or didn't believe a word of it and the strings were rising and rising and she looked at Martin his gentle long face again and saw a mask

a beautiful mask

and every face around her and below her was a mask and all the gilded opulence was meant to hide something

what was being hidden

and she saw a towering curling angry wave of blood gushing out from the stage and breaking across the audience and they were screaming and shrieking with delight because that's what they were praying for

she couldn't breathe and had to rush out of the box

walked up and down the carpeted corridor, avoiding the mirrors, trying to catch her breath. The gas lamps were burning low. Where had that fear come from. It was so horrible. They all seemed in on it but nobody had told her. She thought she couldn't even tell Martin, that it would make her sound mad. She just wanted to forget it immediately.

From behind her, a man approached, asked if she needed any help. Because she couldn't speak she reached out her hand and he held it properly while she leaned against the wall, the wall covered in paper lined with soft velvet stripes.

He was handsome, particularly his mouth. He persuaded her to come outside and get some fresh air. He put his arm around her waist.

My fluent waist.

The lights of the city seemed brighter and more exciting than she had ever seen them. They were real. They were like flags.

Somehow she forgot to go back inside. He was very gentle with her but he laughed a lot at what she said. She took off her shoes and walked barefoot beside him through the crowds and the lights.

Close your eyes, he says to her later, close your eyes and tell me what you see.

It's a room. I'm inside. I'm lying on a bed.

Tell me about the room.

No it doesn't matter. It's only the bed.

What's happening?

Wait. Don't stop.

Who's there?

There's somebody watching me.

Who?

Wait… yes. I'm lying in the bed touching myself. There's a man watching me.

Who?

Nobody. Just a man. Just a little bit harder baby. Yes baby. He's not allowed to touch me you see. Is he masturbating? Is he allowed to touch himself baby?

Yes.

He takes out his big cock and he's wanking. Standing over me. Oh baby there's two of them. They're standing at each side of the bed. They're both wanking. What should I do?

What do you want to do?

Oh no there's more. There's four of them, more. All around the bed with their big cocks out. Looking at me. I have to show them. They're all wanking over me baby. I have to show them. It's all going to pour down on me. I have to make them come. They're doing it hard, really hard, really fast. Oh baby harder. I have to. It's my job. Tell me to come baby. Tell me.

HE DID AS SHE ASKED but afterwards he was very withdrawn. The next day he wouldn't touch her. Then she didn't see him for nearly a week; he was always making some excuse on the phone. His kiss was different when they met, shallow, automatic. They started to argue over nothing. She had her suspicions about what was wrong but couldn't find the right words to ask him.

Now it was him who was afraid.

You've brought this out of me don't you see? she said to him later, as she climbed on top of him. Now it's my turn to show you.

YOU BROUGHT IT OUT OF ME and left me crazy and alone with it, so full of dreams and bursting ripeness and waves that carry me away don't carry me far enough

one more wave and there'll be nothing left of me one more picture of you

and I'll be scattered like foam or a flock of birds all across the sky over the city crying out—one more thought of your body the poise of you your long arms your spine or if the sun comes out and nuzzles my face or a leaf licks my leg or another man looks at me or I smell the river or even the damp darkness in Anna's shop settling on me or the breath of one of the men on my shoulder or the cry of a gull one more touch

scattered like a torn string of pearls

and I wasn't a counterfeit of myself anymore you could hold me up to the light and see the watermark

the hidden face

in me in everything

IN THE DARK I GO OUT into the street. Sit down on the dirty bench. It's wet from the rain and soaks through. I'm wearing only my purple slip with the thin triple straps and the gold hem and the seam stitched up each breast to my nipple. He's on his way, I know he is.

The cold air makes my nipples grow so stiff they hurt. I can smell a thousand stories under the tree. Sorry tales, reawakenings, revenge stories, love duels. I have a pearl necklace wrapped around my wrist. There are leaves stuck to the soles of my feet.

car headlights drown me and they don't dim until I'm blinded.

I can hear the engine stop beside me, hear the door opening.

His voice in the brightness.

I get in.

He is old

He is young
has a voice that makes me feel hollow calling up the flocks in me
out of the caves filling up with water
He strokes my cold smooth strong thighs taming them
reassuring them
The leather is soft under me
I don't want to see.
His hand must go urgently inside my slip and grasp my
breast pressing with his fingers like he is checking it is real.
his mouth at my nipple drinking painfully until I'll never see
again don't need to see again and the car must be moving now
and
he lies me stretched out on the seat and opens my legs
pisses on me first splashing right between my legs
has to take me into his lap and slide up far inside in one
movement and my convulsions
Oh fuck I want him to piss on me

ANNA HAS BEEN LOOKING EXHAUSTED and worried. She moves
sluggishly, wheezing and dizzy between the shop counter and
the cooker. Veronica sits her down and starts to make the tea
which she has never been allowed to do before. Anna barely has
the strength to bring the cup to her mouth. Either she's forgotten
or she couldn't be bothered to put her teeth in. We should call the
doctor, Veronica says.

In response Anna tells a story about the day she was married
and the flowers she carried and her first house.

Do you think I made the wrong choice? she asks when
Veronica gets up to leave.

About what? But I have to go Anna. I have to meet somebody.
There's enough in for the soup under the sink. I'll drop back in
later I promise.

I didn't imagine my life would be like this you know. Don't listen to anybody but yourself, Anna wags a finger at her.

I'll call back in later.

Only Cushty is at the door this morning admiring the cold blue and gold day rubbing his hands with excitement

Never say never, Cushty says and clicks his fingers on either side of her head.

When she comes back that evening, she will see the door of the shop is closed, much earlier than ever before.

In the little square of park, she sits on her favourite bench, an iron bench, black scrolling fern curls for the arm and green wood to sit on. The bench like a gloomy brooch at the intersection of two shady paths. Now and again, to some rhythm she is watching for, the tree branches let go a few leaves. The freshness in the breeze is so young and hopeful it sends the gulls high and mad in the blue sky too bright to watch for long. Behind her is a thorny rose bush. She is wearing a brown corduroy fisherman's cap and one of her long scarves. Passing some time before she meets up with her friend Cathy.

Bear in mind all you've ever been told about why it's important to tell the truth

the sweet musk of the roses advises her that life is not that simple the pretty hem of flowers around the feet of the proud wise tree

A shining boa of chain locks up a side gate to the street and through the bars she catches sight of a black car, a limousine maybe, as it turns a corner and is gone.

Last night she took her suitcases down from the top of the wardrobe—was it last night, or the one before—and set them out on the floor, one, two, three, the lids open like giant oyster shells. She counted that she has packed these suitcases five times in her life.

Cathy is her oldest friend, and still her best friend she would have to say. They grew up together on the same housing estate on the edge of the fields. They practised kissing together, went on their first dates together, often standing shoulder to shoulder or lying in the long grass, checking how far the other would let her boy go with his hands, with his mouth. The night she let Paddy O'Brien slip his hand down into her knickers she looked at Cathy and has never forgotten her red face of amazement and fear. Even so, before they had to go home that night hairy Carl was doing the same to Cathy. From that time on they would go to their own parts of the field, or into the wood.

It was to Cathy's she ran after the party fiasco. Martin was meant to have arrived back but there had been a delay. He wouldn't let her cancel it, he wasn't as fond of parties as she was anyway. All I want is to see you, he said on the telephone. She was so happy, so drunk. She let him talk to Donal and went back out to the garden to dance some more. Much later, when there was only about five people left out in the garden, Donal came out of the house, deeply stoned, his eyes almost closed and his face extremely pale. Veronica grabbed his arm and forced him to dance with her. He is a terrible dancer. She even kissed him on the cheek, slapped him on the arse to make him move with her. She danced around him in circles, begged him to go get his drum, and she would be his spirit. His djinn. That's when he told her.

SHE CAN'T REMEMBER MUCH after that. She must have went wild. She attacked Donal with her fists, threw things around, cups, plates, bottles. She tore up flowers. She was out in the street screaming. There was some scene outside the shop, the lights coming on. Somehow, she must have got a cab that took her to Cathy's because the next morning she woke up in her godchild's bed with toys in her hair. She lied, said there'd been a fight with Donal, nothing more. For two weeks, she stayed out in the suburbs, alone all day in the perfectly tidy house, afraid to mark the floors with her boots or make a dent in the leather sofa, sitting hour after slow hour in a hard chair by the bay window

like she was a doll in a window in some kind of show house

she wanted people to see her and shake their heads but the young families left hurriedly in their cars in the morning and the homes were locked and silent and not even the sun got in and the rippling garage doors

and the lights went on in the evenings and curtains were drawn.

Donal called again and again on the phone. Then one time it was Martin and she forgot everything at the sound of his voice and

forgot everything in an instant and told him to come get her straight away she couldn't wait another second I'm sorry I'm sorry it doesn't matter nothing matters my love

the tone in his voice that got inside her like poison strangling her heart she cursed him coward put down the phone.

It was only a kiss; it meant nothing. How can you be so stupid so suspicious so blind?

He didn't ring back.

She went out for a walk, got lost and found herself at a local garage shop. She bought milk and a packet of balloons for her godchild and asked for the manager. He was a boy of about nineteen. She said she wanted to apply for the job as a cashier advertised in the window. His white shirt was much too big for him, puffed out at the sleeves. His neck was red from shaving. He brought her into the back office and showed her the surveillance camera screens. He put in a tape of the car park at night, people getting in and out of cars, driving off, men and women. He was very excited; this was top secret stuff, he said. Veronica recognised a woman who lived two doors up from Cathy, a middle-aged woman with a car full of children. The young man kept his hands in his pockets. His name badge said Marty. He sat back against the edge of the desk and told her about the job with his hands in his pockets. She wanted to reach out and rub him

lightly rub him while he talked.

She was babysitting and rang Donal. Lost her temper as soon as he answered. He said all he knew was Martin had come back and then vanished again.

Cathy and Paul had been arguing, it was easy to tell, when they came in. Cathy went straight to bed. Paul poured the two of them a brandy. He was aging quickly, losing his hair, putting on weight. He started to talk about when they were all children, about the evenings they went out into the fields, the wood. His life made no sense to him, he told her, it was only responsibilities and duties that held it together. When she went to the fridge for some ice, he came up behind her and put both his hands on her breasts. Like he had been the first to do all those years ago, the first to discover that her nipples sent a wicked shiver down through her to a new place in her and for a while she thought she had two bodies, one of them invisible.

I still think about you, you know, Veronica. Even up there in the bed. You were always the sexiest. We all used to talk about you. Foxy Veronica. You would do anything. You didn't care what people said. Remember the night we broke into the ice cream van? Remember…

He was whispering crying while she stared at the food on the shelves of the fridge, butter, a half circle of bakery apple cake in a silver tray, sausages, a dish of pureed broccoli, baby food in jars. He used to be the sweetest and yet the toughest boy on the estate.

SHE TAKES A BUS INTO TOWN. Skin and stone beyond the glass. A big fat creature of stone and muck and glass

with bones sticking out of it and bits of skin, a sick mixed-up monster sewn together and escaped and the terrified faces are just pores and glass fucking steel and eyes stuck in the concrete and a river for a big cunt sewn up with bridges

and breasts falling off and crawling

and wheels and switches and engines and noise roaring and the light like gas from graves choking and greed and farting and the skin stuck to the glass and digging and drilling and the cranes stitching to keep it alive and greed and greed

and greed and the sun feeding it more and the stitching showing everywhere and ripping

oh my God don't let me turn ugly

SHE HAS TO MEET CATHY in a shopping centre café tucked between two escalators. People are carried conveyed up and down importantly under the glass steeple. The café's metal tables are in a circle around a noisy fountain. It has become a wet lunchtime; people are soaked, steaming, dripping, noisy, impatient. Two younger girls with skin the colour of her milky coffee are talking cheerfully in another language at the next table, some warm sensual language she would love to feel in her mouth, in her ear. A woman in an extravagant white coat and green leather gloves glides to the ground floor on the churning metal teeth, a woman who has never been disappointed, who loved once and won, her red lips have never kissed the wrong man, Veronica is sure she can tell. How do you make love

do you ask him to curse you tie your hands would you let him bruise your perfect skin to take you suddenly from behind do the darker mornings turn you on as you slide your hands into your mint green gloves

Why do some suffer.

In one of the shop windows there is a girl changing the outfits on the dummies. She holds an arm clamped between her legs while fixing the other in a socket. At her feet there is a pile of limbs and two heads with blonde hair. The dummy has perfect round breasts without nipples. Veronica wonders where they found the mould for the dummies, if it is a real girl's body, and then she thinks about her dream, which comes every night now,

her statue dream when the men in the circle fill the bowl with their blood as she stands on the white fur naked

they admire her body she is excited

one of them dances around with a paintbrush dipped in the blood and each stroke of the hot brush along her skin gets a round of applause from the men and each stroke turns her to

stone

Cathy has bought a black blouse with a cute collar she says she needs for a job interview. She looks impeccable, healthy, confident although she complains about not getting enough sleep. Pierce is getting his teeth. Her lightened hair is always brushed back into a simple clasp at the back. She has a pretty face, a sharp nose and quick sceptical brown eyes that suspect a trick or a ruse in everybody. She was like that even as a child after her father ran off with another woman. School was easy for her, the exams, while Veronica had to struggle to remember facts and rules no matter how much she read over them. She works for a solicitor. One thing Veronica knows now however is exactly what Cathy will say when she tells her the truth, about Martin, about Donal.

Cathy liked Martin; he seemed straightforward to her, direct, ambitious. He was good at making people like him. Donal is a different story. The one and only time they met the two of them argued, Veronica can't remember what it was about anymore, something stupid, the name of some album or where some island was, and then when Donal accidentally dropped a bag of grass on the floor looking for money in his pocket, Cathy was outraged, insulted, like he had done it against her deliberately, and she took her coat and bag and left. She refused to come to the party, or anywhere near where people were taking drugs.

Cathy will see the truth in her face, in the pallor of her skin, the pitch of her voice.

So Ronnie tell me all your news, she says lightly, pretending not to be cross for having been ignored these last few weeks, pretending she guesses nothing.

Although it had not been on her mind, Veronica finds herself telling Cathy about the limousine, trying to make it sound funny. Cathy isn't interested at all. She resists it. She purses her lips, shakes her head and forgets all about it. Just one more creep. Most men are creeps. Find a nice one who doesn't want to mess, that's the way Cathy goes. The rest of it all is for teenagers. Be serious.

I got in, Veronica tells her. This catches her attention.

I got in. Don't panic. I just got in and talked to him to see what he was like and then I got out again.

Cathy scowls at her, chewing a mouthful of her tuna sandwich. She is probably thinking back over all the stupid risks Veronica has taken, all the time she's wasted, all the boys she went with, the constant drama and tears.

You hate me sometimes don't you Cathy. You want me to be like you. You're tired of all my confusions and aches aren't you. You think I'm looking for attention. You are a mother now and nothing else matters. I'm so frightened Cathy. So much is happening in me, too much to cope with, like I've split open and all this stuff is pouring out, streaming gushing out.

Cathy he's not coming back.

Her best friend wipes her mouth with a napkin, eyes instantly hardening and darkening like a cat's about to pounce. The same look she gave one time when she caught Veronica snogging her boyfriend at a disco.

The damp gaping frantic lunchtime shoppers go up and

down, in and out, searching

    it is the crowd en masse that will find the answer

    What in the name of God happened Ronnie?

    Cathy there was one time in the woods when I was on a date with Gary, tall ginger-haired Gary who kept the rabbits. We were kissing and over his shoulder I saw this figure behind a tree watching us. It was a man, a grown man. He knew I saw him and he was about to run, waiting for me to tell Gary. But I didn't. Gary went on kissing me and the usual with his hands the way they did and this man started coming slowly closer, from tree to tree. I let him watch, even when Gary's hand went up inside my skirt. But that's not all. I went back in there the next night and I sat down and I waited and waited for him to come back.

    I can't stop thinking about stuff like that Cathy. On the way here, after I got off the bus, I pretended I was following a man in front of me. I was pretending I had to kill him. He had hurt me and I was going to kill him. I wanted to stick a knife in him and see the blood. The rights and wrongs of it didn't matter.

    I am a ghost in a dark house and my body

    is my hot grave.

CATHY PHONED WORK and took an extra hour. They went to a pub, and Veronica ordered a bottle of wine. Cathy wouldn't go beyond the one small glass. Veronica told her the story, she had to tell some parts of it over and over, parts she herself thought were insignificant but that Cathy obviously thought were deadly important, like the way Donal sometimes disappeared for a couple of days or the meals he cooked for her or the night of the party when he brought along a new girl who was too friendly with Veronica, who followed her around, saying I just love your clothes I just love your whole style.

    What the hell are you still doing there? You have to get out of there, Cathy insisted. He's sick in the head that one. I told you Ronnie. He's bad news.

She wanted Veronica to come to stay with her, with us. Pierce would love it, she said.

Explain to me what you are still doing there. Right now. Explain. And what about money? You gave up your job.

I wanted to be ready.

It was a job, it was money, Ronnie.

I hated it, sure you know that. I wanted to think and be ready and clean when he came back.

Cathy shut her eyes put up her hands to block the words. Veronica thought about her husband, his hands on her breasts, weeping for his youth.

First, get out of that house straight away, Cathy was telling her. Today. Tonight. Promise me.

Cathy, I can't. I'm not there. I am there. I'm not anywhere. My body is everywhere and then I'm a ghost. I'm haunting the place and then I want him to die too. I kissed him and he killed me. I am wet all day long with anger. I know he's not coming back and maybe it was me who did it. I gave myself to him and it frightened him away. I am dead and my body has never been more alive reverberating humming like an aching golden chord. My eyes are dry and my thighs are soaking. I have to change my underwear twice a day. I can smell myself Cathy.

the dogs follow me, the old men throw stones at me. The boys start to punch each other when I pass. I want him to see my corpse. He's not getting away with it, what he has done to my love. He said to me there is nothing else but selfishness, the honest selfishness of the flower, of the mountain, and all the rest is junk and talk. There's a burning drum between my thighs pounding pulsing

I don't know what to do Cathy. But I know I can't leave.

THE RATTLE OF COINS LANDING on the bar brings her back to the face of the man on the stool talking to her. A plump white face with wistful eyes. This man's voice she can't hear but it is a small fire warming her face. He touches her shoulder or her knee, gulps his pint. He peeks under the brim of her hat to see if she is listening. She smiles

she smiles sadly. He is one of those men who is inspired by a woman's sadness, attracted to it, he must attack it, he must do what he failed to do as a boy and make his mother smile

stop her weeping.

All the weeping mothers. All the laughing sons.

Where do the daughters swim.

He crooks his cold finger under her chin to raise her face and his lips move. His tongue is folded like a pink leaf behind his stained teeth. She nods reaches for her glass

glass of whiskey and ginger she is drinking now

He squeezes her thigh and leans forward, laughing deeply, near her breasts. The barman is watching, wiping the counter.

Surely this is the same man who asked her for a light earlier. How would he touch her this man. How would he kiss her. His hands are well tended and clean, he keeps stretching and cracking the bones of his fingers. She could drink all night with him, go to a hotel with him and pretend

his incredulous delight as she dances for him

pretend the night away and be whoever she wanted.

She feels his glazed scheming eye on her bare neck, her chest, her mouth, vying for her. He thinks she is on for it. He is growing more brazen.

The barman lifts an eyebrow

a hotel room and her own city outside

to dance for a stranger

Take this man by the hand and show him open his mind

Suddenly she hears music. Over in a corner, a young man with dreadlocked hair is singing playing the guitar. Part of his little finger is missing. He is singing his heart out to the crowded indifferent bar. The song flushes through her in a soft wave, washing it all away

hotels and Cathy and doctors and beds and Martin and shopping and her lover lost somewhere

happily empty for the length of the song

Veronica gave the man one kiss of her one taste. The barman winked in satisfaction to see her go. As soon as she was in the street she bumped into a woman who looked exactly like her mother.

knocked the woman to the ground in the busy street. The woman's bag spilled open into the gutter.

The first time she was taken into hospital you went into her room and stole the necklace of milky pearls from the padded jewellery box on top of the drawers. She adored that necklace; she clung to it like a rosary. You were getting ready for a date. He was older, suave, he had soft black hair like a dog, a tattoo of a flag and he had walked up to you in front of the girls and asked you out. You wanted to wear the pearls. Your mother was in hospital and you robbed her favourite pearls. The walk to meet him in your heels and make-up took you through the estate and down the zigzag alley to the smelly defaced bus shelter on the main road. Your name was written there, woven into the fabric of lies and secrets and angry betrayals.

Foxy goes all the way Foxy swallows Foxy would do it for a chip

But you didn't get there anyway because on your way down the alley a hand went over your mouth and you were pulled from behind and a hand went down your top and grabbed your breast and tried to get up under your skirt

the smell of beer a man's breath a man's hand

and you bit with your teeth into the hand broke the skin and your mouth went warm with his blood

and as you tried to run you felt the necklace pulled tight choking against your throat until it snapped and the beads went flying and scattered and you ran

A FLY SCUTTLES ACROSS HER CACHE OF JEWELLERY like the tangled sparkling innards of some fabulous animal. All the pretty stones and soldered twisted metals and leather and glass she can't wear anymore. Her mirror is a coffin in the shape of an eye. Across the street, through the rain, they are having a party. She has been watching the people arrive, the taxis, the ones with umbrellas or the groups of lads soaked and singing old songs. Many of the faces are foreign, friends of the girl she guesses. A new language would give her a new body.

Her room is an old mouth that has no more words no more kisses

She closes the curtains and undresses in front of the mirror.

my breasts

my hair

You went to the salon to prepare yourself for his return. Make me smooth like gold water cashmere silk velvet a new leaf. A narrow band of fine hair between your legs furry strip just visible. My golden path he called it. Your legs are too short, too thick below the knee, ugly ankles, and your feet you never show.

but your skin is still so soft it delights you. On your arms, your neck, your belly, thighs, buttocks still so soft and firm and healthy. Turning side on, there is a high clean rounded curve to your buttocks. You wish your hips could be fuller.

Your mouth you need to be careful to hide that pain or the corners will go down.

How do I know

The truth her roots are showing like the truth. The honey

blonde and white blonde is streaky and patchy but it's so expensive. She makes a snake of her hair and coils it on top of her head with a ten toothed wooden clasp.

my breasts. Your cross-eyed breasts. They are almost squarish and so soft and pale and kept secret and your nipples can grow to an embarrassing length, so long and tight and taut

two sore hard infant cocks

He put a ring on each nipple, slipped them on. They point away from each other and every man who has seen them

when you show them to a man

they groan with pleasure hypnotised.

Save this body for love alone.

Remember it was like a pity what you felt for his hard cock you beat it with your breasts beat it suck it ride on it

How do I know this is me in the mirror where did I learn

these dreams are my own

hold them up to the light

Her breasts are her two best friends, the only ones who know what it is like to be her.

touch me this body

A man's arm at an open car window

three men at the dark turn of the stairs.

the way you liked him to take you sometimes you naked and him with his clothes on just his red cock out of his zip

do it quick and hard sometimes use me and leave

The curve of your breast in a loose dress as you bend to get into the car

A black car follows you in the rain.

Fuck me fuck me you said to him fuck me like you would that posh girl at the table the night we met fuck me like

Aren't I beautiful for you. Didn't I show you enough. Did I frighten you off.

Come back or this mirror

Hold me up to the light

THERE'S THE DOOR NOW. By the firmness of the hammering she knows it has to be Moore. Surrounded by pillows and cushions, she is lying on her bed. Between his determined bursts of knocking, the voices and music from across the street. Most nights when he calls, she doesn't answer watches him from her window go back up the street to the corner where he stands in the loveless light from the lamp high in the tree, smokes a cigarette, one foot up on the bench like a cowboy. One time she saw a woman approach, they talked and went off together. She thought the woman looked like her. Or the time she saw him pissing in the lane, he leaned against the wall with his left hand, his legs spread, his head lifted to the stars and his mouth open.

She had wanted to invite him to the party for Martin's return, the whole lot of them, Anna, the watchers but Donal wasn't happy about it. He came anyway with Anna early in the evening and was friendly to people, polite. He found an excuse to get upstairs when somebody mentioned the crack appearing on the bathroom wall. He was up there by himself for a few minutes until she was worried about him looking into her room and went up to check. They met at the top of the stairs. He had one hand on the wall and the other on the banister. Her head was level with his groin, which he didn't miss. He said something disgusting. Mentioned her old-fashioned pillow, the roses embroidered. To her relief then, Anna spoke from the bottom of the stairs to say she was leaving, and gave him a look askance to inform him he was too. He can be commanded.

Under her pillow she found a porn magazine. It was open at

a picture of a woman lying on the red carpet of a marble staircase, her legs wide open, shaved, holding her enormous lips open with two fingers, displaying the very inside of her scarlet.

She opens the door to him from the dark house.

The ghosts of me crowd in behind. Let him in. Don't let him in.

She has pulled on jeans and an old V-necked jumper. She is surprised to see it is raining heavily. Moore is drenched. She keeps one hand on the door, laughs. Her laugh is different these days, harsher.

The party's over there, she says. I didn't think much of your taste in wine by the way.

He is in strange humour, distracted and angry. He is not lewd for a change. The rain pounds him trickling down his face but he doesn't notice it. His eyes are like a blind man's. Maybe he is drunk or on something. Feeling vulnerable, she leans out to look at the party house, to remind him there are people near. The thick slabbering rain

the jaws of the night drooling salivating

Anna's not well, he says.

Oh my God. Is it bad? Is she asking for me?

The doctor's been.

Is she asking for me though? Shall I come over?

He shakes his head impatiently, scattering raindrops. This is not the point, he means. This is not what he's doing there in the rain.

She waits to hear what. He is from another world to the faces she can see in the window across the street, the music

from a place of hard thoughts dire unending passions

You'll catch your death, she says. The word seems to incite him in some way, thrill him like he was hoping for her to say it

as if she had said cock or fuck me now

He moves in nearer.

Moore?

You, he says. That's the only word for what he's doing there.

I'm not playing Moore.

He traps her in his stare. There is no escape. The night, the street, the lathering rain are part of it, the bait

he is a hunter

She is purely an apparition of his desire.

Stop it Moore.

He sneers at the idea, that he should stop it or that he would be able to.

Stop it right now.

You know how to stop it.

Rain in his mouth. You don't want this. You don't want to want this. You know what he'll do. Know do want no you

I'm not letting you in, she says. Donal's in.

Again he snarls. But he has no words. He has gone beyond words. He waits there in the rain he has dreamed up.

I have to go. Her hand out of sight crawling up the door to the latch.

He doesn't move. Mucus melting stones. Shimmering puddles of spit in the street lights. The cars like wrapped up carcasses to be eaten later. Cocoons.

Very slowly, she begins to close the door, waiting for his boot to block it.

goes into the darkness of the living room and tentatively puts her head near the side window. His face turns in her direction, violently magnetised. A car approaches, and the headlights emblazon him, his streaming occult face.

Four girls laughing running through the rain from a taxi
and the shallow kitsch music.
and he has vanished
darkness again.

MARTIN TAKING HER, pounding against her, triumphantly. Almost on his knees ramming between her thighs, his arms solid and immovable on either side of her head, his chest above her face

holding on to his chest hair with her teeth

He knows he can fuck her until the world comes true and she is running naked through the streets

He has her owns her controls her.

Please don't stop baby.

Not unless you do what I say.

To demonstrate what he means, he pulls out of her. The streets of the new world vanish. Veronica screams with frustration

a vicious scream of rage that shocks her. My selfish hunger. She claws at his back to bring him back into her. She doesn't want the game to get in the way of her pleasure.

she begs him aggressively hissing fuck me fuck me

he tears back inside her to where she can only go with his help and by getting tighter blocks the way back

Give me more, he says. Give me more than you give him

Who?

Him.

Who?

Your man. Your love.

he wants to play at being the stranger the interloper the backdoor lover

No, she says. Never.

Give me more than you give him or I stop.

She shakes her head and pulls him in tighter she is not far from coming again. He may not know it but he is testing her

No.

Give it to me—show me.

No never.

he stops again and outraged she slaps his back hard twice wants to slap his face

give me more than you give him

she goes for being quiet and can see herself on the street from above while he keeps pressing into her demanding in her ear

Are you giving me more?

she is there now deep inside herself so deep where the roots are the thousand roots straining pulling tight incandescent

hears him, Tell me you are giving me more tell me.

she can't speak she has no mouth nods her head

but it's not enough, Tell me say it or I stop

nods the roots are being torn up, roots into herself and deeper the deep red roots that go down under the earth under the skies below

Say it. Are you?

with a huge struggle yes giving you more

Than him—say it.

yes

defeated he's beaten her, taken his revenge. Afterwards she cries and throws him aside. She lies on the mat on the bathroom floor, trembling. His revenge on her for that phantasy. He knows how to break her. Her man's pride.

I adore you for that pride.

For my hunger.

wants him again as she gazes with delight at her wild face in the mirror.

IT MUST HAVE BEEN THE NIGHT BEFORE that Moore stood in the rain. She doesn't understand time anymore, it has lost its hold on her. Laps around the feet of her statue. From then to now, here to there, it is as hard to know when one kiss stops and another begins so lightly. My inside has spilled outside, she says to herself under the crisp white linen duvet, time is afraid of me, she says also and wishes there was somebody to say this to. Time is for those who have given up feeling in favour of

doesn't finish the thought because she hears a noise, a bathroom noise, ceramic and sharp, scissors dropped in the bath.

She has been awake since before it was light. Before the velvet cloth she bought for the windows changed from darkest blue to a soft purple. Her body is as heavy as stone.

Another noise and she calls his name. Donal. He might have come back during the short time she was asleep. She doesn't remember getting into bed. She is naked. Naked and heavy as a statue in a bed.

Donal.

The room is so old. The new light of the day floating lost in an old room. The fireplace is like a little black font high above the floorboards. Dip your hand in the fire and bless yourself. It's been so long since she's prayed. Dear God, bring him back to me and I promise I will

Now there's a noise from down in the kitchen. A chair. Donal could be down there with somebody. Trying to carry on till the last, always the last, always one more drink. Relentless indifference. No sense of proportion.

That's what she needs to say to him, you have no sense of proportion. When a night has been had and it is time to say it is over and be glad of it. And you are a liar. Your cheap nasty smut.

His total indifference to anybody's pleasure but his own. When you scratch the surface of him. Martin knows when to stop. She used to be able to glance at him and they could agree at the same moment they should leave. Only once he ignored her and she left a party without him, walked by herself and was frightened. A taxi stopped for her although there was already somebody in it. It was a man. He didn't seem to care where he was going. He asked her if she fancied a late drink.

Anna is probably lying in her bed further up the street. She has to visit Anna today, bring her something. What does she like.

That was definitely a chair noise.

I can't move. Where are you now Martin. Are you thinking of me. Come and get me and roll me down the street like a statue knock all of them over the whole city jumping out of the way

imagines herself being found in the bed turned to stone. The crowd in the room. The duvet pulled off. A nubile nude. And they decide to put her on a plinth next to the dirty bench. The men leave flowers at her feet. Violets.

There are times when I know you will not be able to hear me when I call. The sky is thick, clogged, there is noise around you, a crowd of people, girls devoted to helping you through your pain, curled in chairs, at your side in some pub, in the passenger seat of the van, listening to you they say but they are tricking you, don't believe them, don't talk to anybody for by encouraging you to pour out your heart, to go over and over it again, they are beguiling you towards the centre the hollow core where it is all meaningless. Incomprehensible. Where everything crumbles. They know it is words that will kill us. Don't talk to anybody my love. Words are the foe of love.

Utter my name to no one.

Do not pray for us.

Then wait and the sky will clear suddenly, and for the briefest time the secret airwaves will be exposed, the immaculate space, the scintillating tendons

hear me this body I flow humming towards you

The smile vanishes from her face when she hears a tinkling just outside her door. Like bracelets on a woman's arm.

Martin, she calls out. I mean Donal. Donal?

She could swear she hears laughter, low evil laughter.

Who's there?

She can't move a muscle.

Hear me now my love like the time I was sick. I needed you and you came. I heard the horn of your van in the street as soon as I cried your name. Whenever I get scared I see you in the street, the door of your van flapping open behind you as you run towards me, and I am running straight at you in my bed clothes, my sick wear, the grey frayed cardigan and white long johns, barefooted through the puddles. I hadn't washed myself for days.

It was the third month of the five we had together. Spring days of salty rain.

HE SAID HE HAD KNOWN A GIRL who liked to be abused verbally while they were fucking. She made him slap her. She would pray aloud as she sat on him, her hands joined palm to palm between her young breasts. While he hissed at her that she was a slut that she couldn't stop herself that she was the devil's bitch. And as she prayed more loudly he began to shout. You're a fucken slag and you love it and you want your father to give it to you in the arse your big smelly daddy. And to make your mother watch while he does it don't you. She was only seventeen and wanted to grab the devil's horns. And Donal said when he turned her over he found a cross cut into her back, a branded crucifix that she wanted him to press until the blood rose up to the surface and broke the scab

Lick the proof, she had told him.

THE CANDLES DON'T BURN PROPERLY. They keep going out or the flame is too small and feeble. I wish you could hear me. I am sitting here on the kitchen step trying to make you hear me while you are slouched over the table, your head in your hands, a glass of whiskey in front of you. I think it's Wednesday night.

All day she had spent in bed terrified and frozen. When she finally heard what had to be the key in the front door, she rolled herself out of bed and fell on the floor. It was dark again. Donal had gone into the kitchen. She probably shouldn't go down there, she should leave him alone when he's in that state. From where she is listening on the landing, she can hear plates and pots and the racket of the hot water boiler under the stairs, the flame roaring. It sounds like he is washing up.

Back in her room, she pulled on a cotton slip in front of the mirror changed her mind and wrapped herself in a dressing gown instead, pink silk with a lacy collar. She put a clip in her hair looked at herself.

By the time she gets downstairs, he is sitting at the kitchen table, with his head in his hands above a glass of whiskey. The sink is overflowing with suds, running down the cupboards to make a trail across the floor to his chair.

sits down on the single step before the doorway, in the dark hall, well away from him, leaning on her knees. What do you see in your glass. A failed oracle hunched over a measure of

He knocks it back. Only after he has refilled the glass does he notice her. But it might be an act. He lies back in the chair, showing his neck, offering it to the blade of her anger.

I would make sure it was slower than that, she says.

He gives a look of unbearable incomprehension.

She mimics his expression in the dark, then looks down at her toes, ugly toes, which need to be retouched. Cherry toed.

No, I haven't heard a fucken word from him ok, he tells her, he shouts roars at her.

Say nothing Veronica.

He reaches for his dope box. As she watches his hands at work, she is thinking about all the nights they sat there in the kitchen talking. She wants to roll it for him, wants him to ask her. One simple request and they would move beyond the fighting.

Can you not see that.

The suds are popping and collapsing in the sink. She hears a gull, then what might be the response of another one. It might be near dawn or it might be eight in the evening. The light clipped to the bookshelf puts shadows on his face. She looks at the cushion on the big chair which she held hugged in her arms so many hours when they were talking, picking at the old looping tassles, trying to fix the broken zip.

So where'd you go? She has no idea where this question came out of. It doesn't even sound hostile. She has never asked him where he goes.

He looks up at her with overplayed surprise.

Where'd I go?

Where'd you go?

I met your friend Moore up the street. He said you were telling him about me. About how much of a bastard I was and a weirdo and a hippy dope head and if I upset you again I'd have him to deal with.

He's lying. He's having you on. Ignore him.

I don't like being threatened on my own street by a lowlife small-time gangster.

She laughs. Don't be so bloody dramatic. Moore's no gangster.

I know him a lot longer than you do.

He's all talk. He's bragging. Don't be afraid of him.

I know some of the stuff he's done.

Suddenly annoyed, Veronica stands up. I have nowhere to go. Is this about Moore now? Are we talking about Moore now? Don't we have other things to talk about?

She told him far too much that's the problem. Gave him too much. He sucked it out of her and then destroyed her. Laughed at her.

You're enjoying this aren't you? I really think you are enjoying all this.

He shakes his head, shakes it so sadly so hopelessly that a pain goes through her, a stabbing pain. He is lost. This man is utterly lost. She sits again on the step.

her hands, the black and white tiles, the cupboard door under the sink that doesn't shut properly, the table legs with the fleshy hips.

Be careful Veronica. Wait. Don't jump down his throat. Wait. Let him speak.

Did you mean what you said? he has asked her.

The wind shakes the door to the garden behind him.

A few nights ago. That you wanted to stay.

Is he asking me to stay. Does he know I've absolutely nowhere else. But when

When did I say that?

The other night.

She has no memory of it. But maybe he is threatening her reminding her this is his house.

I'm not bloody stupid, she tells him. I know this is your house.

This is what?

Stop torturing me. I want us to talk.

What did I say? I only asked you a question. He lights his bloody joint. His face in the flame is evil. A glowing red smoky eye in his mouth. Moore with the rain in his mouth. Martin's clean long female lips.

Veronica, I came into your room one night, he announces, spewing out smoke.

An ugly dread seeps up through her from her stomach. He has been in my room. It is almost as if she already knows this.

her asleep on the bed, him in the darkness watching her

Why does that not surprise me? she says, trying to control herself. Is that it? Go on. I want to know. I fucken deserve to know.

He agrees, filling himself with smoke again, offering it to her. She ignores him.

What other secrets does he have. Let them out right now.

I came into your room one night. I couldn't stop myself. I don't know what I was thinking. I wanted something but I couldn't do it. Nothing happened Veronica. I watched you that's all. I wanted you, I was going to try to, but I couldn't. I'm sorry.

Her heart didn't relax; there had to be more.

Yes, there's more, he says. I told Martin.

She screams wails shouts kicks fires an ashtray at the wall.

You are sick you know that? Fucken sick. You need help. A sick bastard. Moore should have punched you. You're nobody's friend, not Martin's, not mine. You're a sick selfish bastard. You destroy anything good. Because you can't have it.

She finds herself standing near him, screaming down into his face. She slaps him. Spits at him.

Bastard. Pig. What else?

He swallows, looks up at her, defiant. Her spit on his chin.

What are you what the fuck are you

His eyes leave hers and travel down her neck to her chest. Her dressing gown has fallen open in the madness and her breasts are betrayed to him.

Is that what you want? Do you want to look? Is that what this is about?

screaming this at him, her gown held open like two white wings.

Go on look. They're beautiful aren't they? Say it. They're beautiful aren't they? Say you've never seen more beautiful breasts. Say it.

Say it.

WHEN SHE LEFT HOME for the first time, she lived in a pink cottage by a canal with a man much older than her. He had been impotent for ten years he said until the night she kissed him. He swore it was true. He wouldn't allow her to work and that didn't bother her; she was with him day and night. He was a musician and he had money. She lay in bed and he played the piano, the flute, lots of instruments. She loved him, admired him. But he wouldn't let her out of his sight. You are too sensitive, he said. He knew she was helpless, that if the man came along who knew the right way to look at her across a room, the right time to kiss her, the right angle for her ear, the right smile when she showed him her new underwear, the right time to seize her when she danced for him, she would not be able to resist whatever the consequences.

She left him for a young man who she had known growing up, a boy who had tried to protect her from herself

from herself, from giving herself away to the other boys whenever they demanded it. He fought them off. But he would never touch her. He used to throw her off him in a rage. She fought with him one night and he disappeared. She almost convinced herself he was dead. She made a promise to herself to change. She would wait like the other girls did, wait and dream. She would be good.

The musician sat down beside her on a bus with frost in his beard.

When she met the young man again by chance on the street, he said he had just got out of jail. She clung to him. Every moment he was away from her side was a torture of doubt and jealousy. He was so cruel to her. They lasted only a few months. She saw him later in a gay bar with a beautiful feline boy on his arm.

There were other faces that had faded, that were never even clear to her. Old and youthful faces she studied hard, mesmerised by their strangeness, by the fact they weren't for her, and she could hear the women waiting for these faces inside her.

Then she had gone to dinner one night and followed a man upstairs to the bathroom.

And a few months later, she had been struck by a panic that she had given away too much of herself and took to her bed. She told him she was sick and became sick. He wanted to look after her but she wouldn't let him. He didn't understand. She spent days under her duvet, without eating or drinking. She imagined herself dying. People would ask why and whisper she brought it on herself. She thought her breath was leaving her body and with her last gasp she called his name and heard the horn of his van in the street.

He told her he had gone down the country to escape and to help dig a foundation for a friend's cottage. There were four of them, some in tents and him in the back of his van. One morning he woke early at dawn and walked across the fields to the river. He said he sat on a stone for a while, watching the sun on fast fresh water, listening to the birds waking, and stood up to have a piss. He heard her calling him. It was definitely her. Without telling the others, he got in his van and drove across the country without stopping.

But I only called you a second ago, she said. They were still on the street. He was wearing filthy work clothes and a woollen hat. His trousers were torn at the knees.

That's why I came, he said.

held the suffering pearl lightly between his teeth and she wanted him to tear her out by the root from between her legs.

That was the first time she let him into her arse.

I'm too small there, she said. He held her down.

Love is the depth of me the surface

but the skin divides me from my love

my agony.

His bliss is outside him.

There's no light until somebody sees it.

Love is not a story.

ONE DAY SHE SEES A BALLOON drifting towards her down a street, a yellow balloon with green ribbons and laughing runs into the road to catch it.

That morning she had gone on a whim to have her hair cut. Face to face with herself in the shop mirror, a mirror framed in what had to be pieces of driftwood, she had lied calmly to the half naked girl with her combs and scissors about a boyfriend, about a special occasion.

Like she deserved, the rain was pouring down when she left.

A yellow balloon

Then she saw him. It had to be him. The same denim with the fur collar, always in denim, and the boots with a heel, despite his height. The overgrown messy fair hair, the long stride. His hands deep in his tight pockets like a little boy. It made sense he was back. Somehow she had thought of him walking aimlessly in the desert, stumbling through sand dunes, his foot prints collapsing disappearing behind him. Of course he was home all the time. Why had she not thought of that.

He could have been waiting on her all along.

She decided to follow him. She would find out where he was going, prepare herself and then confront him. Dry off first. To go up to him on the street would be a mistake; he might simply keep walking, leave her standing.

His direction was away from the city centre. They passed the windowless black castle which was being transformed into a nightclub crossed the river and cut through under the glass arch into the old town. Higher up the hill, when they came to streets of narrow grey houses and long gardens, it was only him and her on the pavement. He was walking with a purpose, he was headed somewhere. The rain stopped and patches of blue began to show across the sky, vivid blue like the eyes in his feminine mask of a face. A cat pawed at the upstairs window of a house as the leaves blew by.

When he went into a corner shop she dallied at a bus stop beside an old woman wearing a walkman. Between them was a full-length advert of a woman in a shower, her hands clasped like she was praying. Suds and froth on her golden skin. Washing away the stone. She rotated the bus timetable display like it would decide her fate. A small bald man came down his garden path checked the bolt in his little green gate and reassured went back inside. Anna—that morning the shop was closed. Veronica had knocked and called up to the window. She didn't have the time to investigate further or she would miss her appointment at the hairdresser's. Sometimes she couldn't believe how self-centred she was.

She searched the numbers and names on the display for a sign, dared some force to direct her. Before there was an answer she saw Martin come out of the shop tearing open a chocolate bar. Martin and his sweet tooth. He often left their bed in the middle of the night jumped in his van to look for a treat for them. Joy filled cleansed her heart. What did it matter what she looked like. There he was now. My king. She was running towards him.

Martin?

He carried on up the street, a steep street where there were cones and signs and men digging up the pavement and smoke and fumes of hot tarmac. He went out of sight behind a little steamroller. The men watched her as she ran. She couldn't help herself smiling. They cheered.

He had turned on to another street by the time she caught him. Out of breath, bent over, laughing, she called his name as loud as she could. Then again as though she was singing it. For the sheer pleasure of it.

At last he stopped and looked back.

It wasn't you. Even in the way you turned your head I knew it wasn't you. Even with the moving cloud behind your face and the flash of sunlight and a rain so fine it was invisible and a rainbow somewhere and the hills, the brown hills that teach you there is not enough time, it wasn't you.

Grieving, cursing herself for believing, she walked about in that unfamiliar part of town. The wind had sharp points in it. Something had happened, she was thinking. She felt a change in herself, a glimpse down into herself, into the possibility that she might get through all this and grow and be happy. Outside a pale stone house turned into an elegant hotel, she toyed with the idea of going in

take a long bath and lounge on the bed and the old furniture would solace soothe her with all the strange and secret things it had seen.

tell me more dressing table. Tell me more waterfall painting in your gold frame.

lie in the bath and wrap herself in a dressing gown while she makes herself ready to go down to the bar where she will sip a cocktail in the low light and plan how to spend the suitcase of money under the bed.

a man will approach. His voice will be like a caress, his eyes like a game she knows how to play

There was nothing to stop her, only herself. She was almost happy, yes, she was happy, it was still there, alive in her, like that little bird up there in the bare dripping branch singing. For the first time in as long as she could remember, she was glad to be the woman she was.

So when the yellow balloon comes floating towards her down the street she runs towards it laughing to catch it.

She would carry it home.

Before she has gone very far with the balloon in her arms, she comes upon two men under a big colourful umbrella. One holds a spray of balloons and the other shakes a bucket at her.

The one that got away, they say in unison.

You're not getting it back, you can do what you like.

The man shakes the bucket at her again.

The collection is for an open day at the animal home which lies at the end of a whitewashed lane behind a tall wooden gate topped with razor wire and balloons. Because it has been a day of surprises and small revelations so far Veronica decides to let herself be guided. Two clowns are kissing in the reception area. They point her towards a bleak corridor which takes her out the back of the building to the rows of dog cages. There is a card on the door of each cage. Her favourite is a brown and white mongrel with spaniel ears called Toasty. The card reads: Hello, my name is Toasty and I love toast, especially the crusts. I am two years old. I was locked up in an attic for a long time so I can be very shy. But I am house-trained and good with children. I need a home with a garden and a high wall because although I'm small I like jumping over things. I can jump over anything. Take me home with you and I'll show you.

Hunkering down, Veronica talks to Toasty for a while, telling him she wishes she could take him with her but she has a bit of a problem with accommodation at the minute. She promises to come back and get him one day soon. In his cage, Toasty rolls about on a piece of flowered carpet between two armchairs and an old portable black and white television with a coat hanger for an aerial.

Further along she comes to an area where the game is you have to guess how many kittens are playing among the shrubs and plants behind the glass screen. Next is a larger cage with some children kneeling inside it, three of them and a bigger boy with his hood up.

A woman sitting at the door of the cage explains that it is a competition to see who can sit still as a rabbit for the longest. The woman then casts a bad look at the older boy, says he's been there three hours already and hasn't flinched. He's spoiling it for the younger ones, she says. Veronica recognises him as the boy she met in the indoor market, the one who Moore called a thief and chased away. At the same time, the two men who were collecting outside come into the cage and lifting the boy under each arm, they carry him out with his legs bent up under him. Veronica follows them out with her balloon. They sit him on the curb. Again, he won't speak to her.

And why the hell should you? she says and decides to take him home.

Skinny and filthy. Skinny and mute. Hungry and suspicious. Pale. Cold deep in his bones. Musty smelling. So thin and battered. When the hood comes off, his hair is fawn and curly. She has sent him up to take a shower.

The balloon floats up to the ceiling while she finds a frying pan and cooks him an omelette with the eggs and bread they bought on the way back. She makes a pot of tea. She hopes Donal is lying in his bed wondering what's going on. The flame of the immersion is roaring in the hall. She opens the door to the garden, goes out and stands in the wet grass, the rubbish, looking at the flowers she planted. She has a picture of the boy cleaning his fingernails, scrubbing them obsessively under the sprays of the water, his entire body, every muscle tensed with concentration. The curtains in Donal's room are closed as usual. She wants to throw a pebble up at the window just for the sheer hell of it.

This is a good day. The first. I'm ok today. I don't have to collapse.

She goes back in and finds the boy standing naked on the kitchen tiles. His face is blank, vacant. For his slight build he has a long ruddy cock and it is hard.

Ignoring him, she goes to the cooker and inspects the underside of the omelette. Does he think this is what he has to do in return for kindness.

He is standing right behind her now.

Veronica turns round and opening her arms she brings his head into her chest.

It's ok. You don't have to do anything. You're safe here with me.

The balloon nudges the dusty yellowing ceiling.

A key turns in the front door, it opens and Donal steps into the house with plastic bags of shopping. A leaf blows in behind him. She holds the boy's head tightly so he can't look around to see. Donal puts down the bag, stops for a moment to take in the scene.

her by the cooker with the naked thin body of a boy in her arms.

a teapot a balloon

He's too far away to read his face. He steps over the bags and goes upstairs. The boy is trembling in her arms, nuzzling his face against her breasts.

It's ok. You're safe with me. Shall we go up and get warm in my lovely bed.

WHEN SHE WAKES, the boy's not there. The room is pale in the centre and dark in the corners.

searches for the smell of him on the pillow. His young starved hard body. Wanting inside her too quickly, so eager. So rough. Biting her lips. Holding his cock with both her hands.

Her eyes open only slightly. The room is a hollow shell like when you suck the yolk out of an egg with a straw. Stretching to full length, she moans. She's horny. His young body was between her thighs

her thighs almost as big as his ribcage. It was so real.

moans and stretches again and rolls onto her stomach, then onto her back again. She'll never sleep in this state. Her hand goes down across her belly, dragging her nails, and down between her legs. The other plucks and plucks lightly at her nipple.

She kicks the duvet aside and opens her legs, looks down to see her own hand at work. It has always turned her on to watch her own hand. Now the darkness in the room seems to slowly tighten around her like a black sail she is pulling winding in

Martin and me sailing that one weekend his eyes melting in the light off the water

coming in at dusk over the golden and crimson band of the sun across the water and the screaming gulls at the harbour entrance and the seals

Look, the watermark he said with his arms around her waist, kissing her neck under her hair

she arches her back

like a door opening a black car

when he used to watch you arch your back like that for him

your soft white body in a tightening skin of darkness a black silk hammock

her eyes flutter open briefly and she sees a shadow between the windows, a man's shadow. She drops her back on the bed. Donal's come into her room again. He's been watching her.

I know you're there Donal. I can feel you there. Do you like it. You like watching me. This is me by myself. Shall I carry on pretend I don't know. I'm going to go on oh yes and show you. There see how wide I'm open. Can you see there in the dark. Come closer. I'm going to show you what you can't have. Can't have. Look, now.

In a second she has come, rolling on the bed with her hand trapped between her thighs. Cursing him.

Look what you made me do.

She sits up ready to shout at him. Bastard. He is right at the bottom of the bed and he is holding out his hands to her and his eyes

his eyes are pouring blood gushing out blood all over the bed.

The rest will be good for you.

I'll be long enough dead, Anna says. I've never liked doctors anyway. Hospitals and sickness. My husband was a doctor. Well, he started out training to be a doctor but he never finished. Money was the problem. And me of course if you were to ask him. I wanted to move to the city. I wanted to see more of life.

Anna laughs unkindly at the memory of herself.

Did you not want him to be a doctor?

It was all in his head sweetheart. Either about me and other men or becoming a doctor. He wanted us to move because he thought I was in love with another man.

Were you?

I never stopped him doing anything. He stopped himself. He never felt he was good enough. I blame his own mother. She...

Veronica is there in Anna's bedroom before the ambulance arrives. They packed her hospital bag together. Veronica ironed her nightdresses on a towel laid across the top of the big dressing table with its mottled three-piece mirror draped with different rosaries

listening to the older woman's nervous talk about her past and her husband and nodding at the pictures of the mass cards she takes out from a dilapidated prayer book under her pillow.

The flower print has dissolved into the wallpaper in the musty room. The orange bedspread feels wet when she sits on it, the bed high off the ground. On the windowsill the dried insects are like bits of jewellery. It's such a lovely soft golden autumn day, they've both said more than once. Seeing the men down in the street, Cushty and McGrory and Eyck, Veronica starts to cry suddenly, helplessly.

The two women sit on the bed, their arms around each other.

I'm sorry, I'm being so selfish, Veronica says.

It's no matter sweetheart. They're only tears. They've never harmed anybody.

Anna begins to say a prayer, the Hail Mary. This is how Moore finds them when he pushes in the bedroom door. Veronica smiles up at him warmly, forgetting herself, glad to see him. His face is red and healthy like he's come from a long walk. He waits for the prayer to end and gives Anna his usual hug. Veronica has to check herself from lifting her arms to be held in the same way. He moves around the room, takes up a variety of poses, leaning against the wall with one hand, his arms folded, hands in his pockets with his head down. Hadn't Anna said to her once, the only way to see a man truly is when he has his head bowed.

Moore keeps them talking, keeps them laughing,

the two of them giggling on the bed hand in hand like girls. Not once does he ruin it and look at Veronica in the wrong way. She is impressed by him, that he knows how to behave at a time like this. Finally Cushty is heard calling up the stairs that the ambulance is on the street. Moore takes the small case and goes down. At the window, Veronica watches Moore pointing a finger into Eyck's face, and the way he seems to be warning the rest of them to behave themselves. The day is so golden and dying already.

There was another golden day when she had watched from an upstairs window, refusing to come down, as her own mother was put into an ambulance

for the last final time. Her heart was broken when she couldn't find the pearls. She lay in the room in the dark for days. You lied and lied and said you didn't know.

As they are about to go downstairs, Anna puts something into Veronica's jacket pocket and makes a scolding face that she's not allowed to look.

The ambulance men have the wheelchair ready out in the street in the sunshine. Moore promises he will look after everything. The other men wish her the best in their own ways. She has a funny word for each of them. Veronica hugs her a last time and says she'll be in to visit her the next day.

Anna whispers to her, You are already true, sweetheart.

The metal ramp rises up, lifting Anna in her chair off the ground. One of the men starts to laugh. Then everybody does.

The ambulance goes off without the siren.

Veronica has already reached the tree when she hears Moore calling her, from not far behind. She stops, waits for him. She feels exhausted. She wants to go back and get into bed and sleep and no dreams. Straight out Moore asks her if she will come for a meal with him that night.

I'm not in the mood. I mean it.

He says, And what will you do instead eh? Sit in that house by yourself? It's not good for you... have the look of somebody who needs a bit of company. You've lost all your... and colour.

He hasn't noticed the change in her hair. She nods wearily. He is right. Up in the tree branches above them there is no help, leaves and branches splitting into twigs, no destiny or truth. The dirty bench is like a shell, a jewel in the clear light.

It'll do you good, he says.

And there's Donal now coming up the street right on cue; she thought he was in bed, that she heard him last night in the kitchen late with somebody. There was music. Moore glances back and spots him too. He grits himself.

Donal looks haggard. Veronica tells him about Anna while Moore keeps his back to him, keeps himself between them almost, staring into her face. She is so tired.

three of them standing in an awkward silence under the tree. Smell of river sluggish rank air.

I'm so tired, she thinks she says. In her pocket her hand brushes against something smooth. It's what Anna gave her, a small black box with a ring in it. A thin silver ring with a small star of emerald stone.

holds it out to the two men like it is the perfect symbol of all she is feeling

watches the faces of these two men their eyes their mouths

looks along the empty street and wants yearns to see Martin striding along it his head moving from side to side slightly with each step hands in his pockets

you already are true

Moore has reached out and taken a hold of her arm. Says, You alright?

Behind him Donal peers at her, asking her something with his wet eyes.

You alright Veronica?

I HAVE WAITED FOR YOU. I have waited when you were coming and gone on waiting when you said you aren't coming anymore. I have listened to every sound on the street at night, the footsteps, the car engines coming nearer, the coughs, the fox at the rubbish bags even the women's heels imagining stupidly imagining you might be trying to trick me and gone on listening to the morning and the whole huge empty day with all its sounds and false alarms and signs and secrets I can't tell you

and every object jealous of every object because it knows what it has to do that day and forever the kettle the chair the table the pillow my shampoo bottle and will never feel this

in somebody's hand

the streets the bars the shops the chapels the parks all there so people won't feel this

the banks and the children

sometimes I feel I have made love to every man who ever lived

and the sky and the make-up

my open thighs and my beautiful breasts and my feet and my love

THE HEAT OF THE FLAMES is burning her. Her eyelids seem to have melted away. She rocks in and out of the heat, dipping her face in through a hot mirror a hot border and in up to her shoulder and breasts and out again feeling her skin contract again crinkling. Her lips are numb. Even her hair is hot. My pupils must be swollen to their limit. As a child she used to be able to do this for hours and float away, hours would pass, spitting into the flames

what were her dreams then until her mother would drag her away and throw her on the street dizzy and drowsy and dopey and sleepy and giddy and foxy the swirling air

dipping her face in the mirror there's a smouldering luxurious red-lighted room on the other side a red sofa plush red walls but her nipples have a precise point of pain that sends her back

behind her the bent white room of a cruel brittle house and the black shell of darkness behind her and the black chimney and the grate like an old brown crown and the two glittering peacocks. Her heart beating like a little drum of delicate skin. If her blood moves faster in the heat will time pass more quickly will she age rapidly skin wrinkle and hair turn to cobwebs before this night is over

this night is every night

darkness behind her put your ear to the black shell of darkness and listen

gusts of howling lonely love

Moore shouting through the letterbox

She took off her top her bra and sat down before the fire

After he had gone into her ass in the dunes Martin jumping nude in his boots from rock to rock along the shore with the horizon for a hat

her hands crushing the sand

The boys shouted filth through my letterbox and my mother shouted down from her bed to ask what was going on

the sea dancing around him flashing her underwear

Remember what I showed you one morning that you said changed your life, me on the chair remember, one leg up, making myself come while you ate your breakfast and the little warm pool I left in the shallow of the chair

he lifted the chair poured it into a glass and drank, toasting the world with your golden juices

What are you going to do Veronica

A statue rolling down the street

The car door shuts the black car drives away but there's a piece of red velvet trapped a tuft sticking out and she grabs hold of it and pulls and the door opens and

the heat melts away all the images and there's just pure desire pure as loneliness

all I am is a woman

she spits into the fire for that fierce blissful hiss she has always delighted to hear

Veronica, listen. Just listen to me for a minute.

Who. Donal's voice behind her out of the black shell. Are you there?

Yes.

How long has he been there.

I thought you knew I was here.

Tries to open her eyes, or were they open, and sees a forked flame trying to tear divide

I didn't know you were there. Are you there?

Veronica listen. I can't stand this anymore. I'm going away.

He can't go away. It's a trick. He can't go away.

I'm serious.

Is he leaving you too.

What do you mean? Away?

Travelling. Anywhere. I can't take this anymore. The atmosphere.

The atmosphere? she laughs.

What does he expect. Throw another party and it's all better. He has been there watching you, your naked back, your hair in the firelight, and it's made him want to go away. He's running away. All of them cowards.

I'm not running away.

You can't leave me alone. Not after what you've done.

You can stay here in the house. Don't worry about that.

I don't care about your house. I hate your bloody haunted house. I hate the dreams I have in your house. I hate you.

So I'll go then. It'll give you a couple of months to sort your head out.

She wants to laugh until the fire shrinks away in shame. Till she sorts her head out. Where is it they travel to when they are all blind. The kingdom of the blind. They moan and fight and tramp about in the desert and don't know it's a paradise around them.

You can't go. Not yet anyway. This is your fault. You're a coward. You're all cowards.

The firelights flits and flicks and bounces up and down the walls like the hem of a big whirling waltzing skirt.

Crossing her hands over her breasts, Veronica turns around on the cushion to face him. Are his eyes bleeding. Are his eyes like bleeding holes for horns.

There he is, just out of reach of the firelight. Sullen shadow man on the sofa. His indifferent sunken sprawl. She says, Tell me I'm mad. I don't want this to be real. Tell me I've gone mad in the head. Do you even care what happens to me?

She watches him stand up, all the commotion of him. Bones and metals and grunts. Don't walk out that door and leave it like this.

He comes towards her, down on one knee, then the other. His worn face in the light now, level with hers. The deep wet smooth textured eyes. The powerful nose. His mouth surrounded by little hairs. The hair crawling up his neck.

the weight of her breasts in her own hands, the fire on her back like ten thousand velvet whips lashes of hot piss

I think about nothing else, he says.

Than yourself you mean?

He hangs his head.

Don't do that, she shouts at him.

He straightens his neck, chastened.

Don't do anything, she tells him. Don't say a word.

Veronica closes her eyes takes her hands away from her breasts. The darkness is a rich emptiness, black as a limousine on a country road in the dead of night.

What do you want? she says. Do what you want to me.

For a long time, he refrains. Don't think or talk or ask. Touch me. I want you to take me. My breasts are burning. Look at me. My hands are locked behind my back, fingers crossed to the sly flames.

The first touch is to her nipples with the back of his hand.

by pushing against her shoulder lies her down, kissing her stomach while he undoes the button of her jeans, her zip

spit into my mouth

piss on me

slides her jeans down over her hips then pulls them off by the ends licking the soles of her feet

torture me

Don't think or talk.

my purple knickers he sneaks them off I am naked now so wet

Let me run away chase me far away

I am in the back of the car

But he seems to have stopped. Do something. Don't gloat over me. Take me. Irritably, she opens her eyes finds him above her staring across her body into the fire. He is burning my knickers.

Then with the shadows grafting legends across his face he grins at her like the devil he is.

She grins him one back

I didn't know I had it in me.

Open my legs so he can see right up inside me smell me.

He takes it out, his head bowed over his cock, scooping out her juice and smearing it on himself.

I'm sorry my love.

A SLIM ROOT OF PLASTIC TUBE breaks through the mottled skin of
Anna's arm. Her bed blanket is green. The stiff white sheets are
folded sharply under her arms. Her hands lie palm upwards, the
skin is strangely pink and smooth, the lines in the process of
erasing themselves. Between her thumb and forefinger a sagging
wing of skin. Slightly swollen joints of her ringless fingers. The
other five women in the ward are moored to the wall with tubes
and wires. Like a tranquil white harbour. Voyage to the other
side. The big windows show them the rough seas of the city they
have travelled across, and the hills faintly misted, the green and
brown bare hills,

the flanks and hairy curves of the giant, where the giant fell,
the fallen giant they chased her into the ground, her face lost like

beheaded they took off her head for her badness but her
blood spilled out like pearls and seeped down into the ground
and formed the rivers and the people drank in her hunger.

And they built their cities of hunger never to be satisfied and
that is the giant's curse. Until they find her head and reunite it
with her body. So they search for the head and

Staring out the fourth-storey window, across the car park and
the cranes, these are Veronica's thoughts as she waits for Anna to
waken from her doze. They have washed and brushed her hair.
Her slackened face gives her an entirely different expression of
startled innocence. One of her rosaries hangs over the head of the
bed. A card showing two purple butterflies on the bedside table

turns out to be from Moore. His handwriting is slow and careful, studded with holes where the pen point broke through the card when he paused to think of the next word. Pressure points. The other women are reading magazines, catching up on what is glamourous and new. Three nurses talking in the corridor, plastered in fake tan. Wearing the green emerald ring, Veronica takes the old woman's hand.

Anna, I stayed in his bed last night. Donal. We hurt each other. I thought we were going to murder each other. I scratched and slapped and bit him. He was bleeding. I wanted him to tear the skin off me and make me into one of his drums. I was screaming and spitting at him. He held me down by the hair. My neck is aching. Every muscle of me is snapped. I thought he'd bitten off one of my nipples. They were bleeding. My mouth was filled with his blood too. But I wouldn't let him stop. I hit him when he tried to stop, I actually hit him because he stopped. He went out of his mind too. I wanted so much I was terrified. I sat on him, right up on his face, screaming down at him, pissing on him, trying to drown him, screaming at him. I pissed on him and he was laughing, gargling it. It's all mixed up. But it was beautiful too, it was. I could see inside of everything, right into the heart of everything like I was God. But it was so violent and beautiful. I'd never felt that before. I made him bleed, Anna. We wanted out of our skins. I didn't care if I couldn't come back. I was going to be a flower or a pearl or a candle flame or a tree or somebody else entirely. Then I don't remember. I was in my own bed when I woke up. Dried blood under my fingernails, and streaked all over me. I could barely move. I had to sit down in the shower.

Moore comes sauntering in with a word for each of the elderly women who sit up in their beds and cast him admiring looks.

He rolls his eyes at Veronica, sits and shakes his head at Anna.

You'd think butter wouldn't melt eh? And where were you last night eh...? Sneaking out when they... lights out.

What are you on about Moore? Let her sleep.

On about? She paid me a visit last night. Talking to me for ages... at me practically. Giving out to me. Madcap stuff I'm telling you.

He looks tired, wound up.

Giving out about what? In a dream?.

He shakes his head bites his lip angrily. If that was a dream then I don't know what. She was raging at me. Stuff from years back. And you were mentioned.

He carries on for a while talking but she can't understand him at all.

I don't have a clue what you're saying.

He leans in, placing his elbows carefully on the bed. A room. Corpses hanging by the neck. An abattoir. Blood pissing out of her eyes and she's still giving out to me. Understand me now?

I'm sorry.

Turn you on does it?

Don't start.

You look flushed.

Veronica seizes Anna's hand for protection.

I'm right aren't I? It turns you on. Is that the kind of thing you're into then is it?

You are disgusting.

You'd know all about that.

I'm not sitting here with—

Moore sits back suddenly, whistling to himself. So I went round to your place this morning didn't I? That miserable house. And what do I see? That spoilt toerag deadbeat there doing the housework. Scratches all down his chest.

And you were there shouting through the letterbox last night as well, Veronica goes back at him. Like some spotty youngster.

I'm at... limit here. You think... isn't that it? Aren't I right? I could give you whatever you want. Whatever you want. I'm telling you. You name it. This is the limit do you understand me. Don't say... lightly... you... final... Anna... mean

Be quiet, she's waking up, Veronica orders him, and realises those are her own tears falling onto Anna's hand.

Moore grumbles some stern words back to her that she doesn't understand.

SHE STAYS ON THE BUS beyond her stop gets off in the city centre. It's been ages since she's had a walk around the shops, nothing in particular to do, passing the time. Every so often she stops abruptly and scans the street behind for a glimpse of Moore. Or she lingers in the most female parts of the shops where he wouldn't dare enter. He won't give up he says. He might have taken to following her. But whether or not he drives himself to distraction over her, the reason she doesn't rush back to the house is she wants to make some sense of her morbid feeling of dejection. Worthlessness. She needs time to think. Absorb what has happened. Him too. Give him a chance to tidy the house finally. It's a good sign surely. Midday in the old city at the start of autumn. The pavements are wet. Gulls gathering overhead in the faintest grey sky. Some streets are completely deserted. She stops at the window of her favourite jewellery shop where she brought Martin more than once to remind him that if he ever wanted to buy her anything, this was the place. Today the rings and necklaces seem cheap and crude. Where are the feelings that delight in these bits of glass and metal. Only one sentiment in her this autumn morning, a woe she calls it,

a sour extravagant woe full of words laws exhortations: Throw yourself in front of that car and have done with it, you will always be alone, that hunched man playing his harmonica for change is a better person than you are, that woman with her pram and baby knows a kind of happiness you will never see deserve.

Exhausted, she finds a café takes a seat by the window. The waitress is foreign and unattractive; they have the same highlighted hair although Veronica's is much longer. A row of flower boxes on little wheels cordon off a few empty tables from the street. It is so pathetic, she thinks, it annoys her so much, these trivial little divisions, it annoys her so much she wants to get up and leave, run out there and push them down the street. Where would you go then, Veronica. The streets are runny stains on the window. They are blunt knives. Scissors that don't cut. She doesn't know what she means. Orders coffee and finds some pleasure in pressing her palms against the warm glossy earthenware. A twisting talon of steam clutches over the edge of the thick rim, then dies, clutching for what. The only other customer, a young man with dreadlocks, closes his book and puts his head in his hands. He is missing part of one of his little fingers from below the knuckle. A guitar in a black case covered with scribbled signatures. Veronica feels sure she has seen him before. Two waitresses preparing the tubs of sandwich fillings for the shelves inside the glass counter chopping onions slices of bleeding tomato mixing egg yolk and mayonnaise with their hands in see-through plastic gloves. She looks at her own hands revolted. Her skin is raw. Her rings are hideous. Who are you kidding, the woe laughs at her. She feels sick. Like her mother, always sick. For so many years, the woman lay in bed, refusing to open the curtains, coughing, shouting, going grey, dying. Veronica had to be dragged in to sit beside her on the lumpy bed. What's wrong with you Mammy. Pray with me Veronica. I stole your necklace so a man came to grope me in the zigzag lane. I bit him till my mouth filled with his blood. I went back the next day found some of the pearls in the dirt only some of them. She played in the lifts when her father took them in to visit her in the hospital. On the night they buried her, Veronica was fifteen. She went out into a car park with a boy to smoke her first joint. He took a piss against the wheel of a car, his back straight, his hands on his hips, whistling. Quickly, she took off her knickers, sat up on the dewy bonnet and let him inside her as they blew smoke into each other's mouths.

She wants to go to the toilet to stick her fingers down her throat. On a wall across the street she reads some grafitti:

Jenny J.P Mick Stash Dervla

out of it

together again

fight to be useless

Smile—we're all forgeries.

Blessed is the beast.

She's in the mood to write some herself, obscene words on a corner wall. Angry uncouth dirty and violent. Look me in the eye as I suck you. An ugly little man interrupts her thoughts as he sits down at a table too near her. The lunchtime crowds are pouring into the streets like spiders from the cracks. She is turning to stone again can't move.

spiders will run over her face like a gravestone statue. Now another man is eyeing her up, Mr Moustache, before he bites into his sandwich. The other little man is wiping his glasses clean. Come and take all the little dreary men. Gag me with your cheap ties. The dreadlocked youth has vanished. Woe says, Look at the steam hissing from the coffee machine and the webs of it creeping across the ceiling and the window fogging

listen to the noise of chairs dragging and squeaking cutlery and glass and metal shoes coats zips the voices the false voices. How is it possible to be so alone. She is not one of these people anymore. I will haunt the streets with a head of cobweb hair and a harmonica. Flashing my tits in the park in a pink nightdress.

Chatting up bus drivers. The light has changed. It is barren now. I feel barren, rotten. Why do they make so much noise these people so busy talking about what. Every word is an ugly little featherless bird smashing against the window.

As though the sky has turned black at that thought, and the ground starts to bubble and burst, she is stricken with a cold terror. Way down inside her a crack opens with the sound of a bone breaking. She dreads her own next breath clasps her arms around herself like she is ruptured coming apart and gapes around the café helplessly at the faces for they must have heard it too. They are stuffing their mouths and chewing and blathering in blind ignorance. They probably wouldn't believe this kind of thing went on in their midst. A crack, what are you going on about. Stay calm Veronica. Don't panic. She waits, holding her breath. For a moment there is stillness, the crack seems to have closed over, everything will be ok. Slowly she begins to loosen her arms releases a gentle breath. It's passed hopefully, whatever it was. Then out of the blue some man claps his hands behind her and it starts again this time more strongly a crack widening opening tearing smoothly

coming toward her a fissure and this time it's not going to stop she is splitting open can none of you see

Somebody does. She seizes on a pair of eyes looking at her quizzically. It's a girl. Her eyes are oval and kind and alive and the palest brown. Looking at Veronica over the shoulder of a man who is talking eagerly to her, who she has to glance at now and again to show she is listening. Keep those beautiful exotic eyes on me. Don't leave me alone whoever you are. The girl's hair is different ragged lengths dyed a lobsterish colour but the roots are black and there's electric blue at the tip of her fringe. Brown skin and little butterfly eyebrows. So beautiful and natural. Just look at me that's all I'm asking. Gentle eyes. She can see the fear in Veronica's face. I'm clinging to you. Even when she speaks to the man she keeps her eyes on Veronica. She has a silver stud in her tongue which sends a tremor of joy into the crack and slows down the splitting miraculously. You're holding me together sunny angel. Your soft fresh gaze. The girl seems to almost nod her head that she understands. The man continues to talk to her. You are saving my life.

There are tears in both their eyes.

The girl made the man delay as long as she could shrugs when she has to leave. While he was paying she stood at the door smiling at Veronica, compassion

have you too sat like this in a café coming apart turning to stone

blinking the tears out of her eyes. Veronica tried to give her back all the gratitude she could summon into her face. They left and a few minutes later Veronica went out also, knowing exactly what she should do. She would never let herself feel so alone again. She waved down a taxi. It wasn't the time for dawdling. She was going back to his house.

hoped he hadn't showered and gone back to bed still smelling of last night, blood caked on his lips and that smell of them like under the tree,

got out of the cab and ran wanted to inhale deep into her fill all the cracks with that smell from him and lie her head on his chest. She had so much to show him if he could only

see

The bin was stuffed with shiny black rubbish bags.

The dishes had been washed. The garden cleaned up.

The note on the kitchen table said simply:

Veronica

I'm leaving now. I haven't decided where yet.

Please stay on in the house. Whatever you want.

If I'm wrong, then I'll be the one who lives to regret it.

Donal.

Below he had added:

Hold us up to the light.

a scuffed bloody fingerprint on the corner of the page.

and a plain gold ring without its stone

I GO OUT THROUGH THE FRONT DOOR into the darkness. There seems to be so much of it—it is vast and so rich and I am so deep inside it. The cold air teems across my skin, my bare arms, my neck and throat. But not against my face. I've painted on a thick mask. My loose hair hangs perfectly. My lips are a moist wanton glossy scarlet. I walk in a cloak of scent. The only sound is my heels on the broken pavement

wrap my coat around me, belt it, yes, there is a belt with an enormous playful buckle. The coat reaches to the ground, sweeping up the dead leaves. Aren't the lights like overgrown pearls glowing luridly. Isn't the city huge and yearning naked apart from a long string of pearls.

white beads red beads

I sit on the dirty bench and wait.

smell of rotting dark in my nostrils

Before long I hear the footsteps. A man's step, exactly how I imagined it. A man walking purposefully but not in a hurry, never breaking his stride. A man who is confident there is nothing will get in his way. Not this night, not anymore.

and all the pearls on the necklace seem to tremble slightly.

He stops directly in front of me. I lower my eyes. His boots are dirty, torn at the toe to show the metal toecap. He doesn't speak. I hold the moment for as long as I can before I look up into his face.

I know it will be Moore. He is wearing a tweed suit.

He offers his hand helps me to my feet. Front and back, I see him slyly inspecting my figure, the cut of me. I feel elegant and powerful. My body is so warm and soft and generous, my exquisite curves glimpsed in the shadows of my coat. His furious wordless desire excites me, his seriousness, his shyness. He offers his arm.

We walk together along the street, shoulder to shoulder. Our one shadow moves before us, extends grows on and on before us like a tree, and we are trying to climb to the top.

At the entrance to the lane we stop.

I stop. I stop him.

The lane is completely dark. More of that sleek flawless darkness. I look at him suggestively, without a hint of shame, to tell him this is the place and he is surprised shocked for a moment. He tries to stop me. I step forward first.

Halfway down the lane, we reach the ghostly shimmer of the metal garage door. I position myself against it, undo the buckle of my coat

the big fat round buttons one by one, open my coat. His hands go in around my waist, sliding across the silk. The satin chiffon foulard. He pushes my hips firmly back against the metal door.

the lock rattles and I can smell the innocence of rust. He goes to press himself against me but I put one hand on his chest to prevent him. My other hand, the palm of my other hand I press hard against his groin. He is not hard yet, not fully. I push him against the door now as roughly as I can

kneel down in the mucky lane.

I kneel down.

Inch by inch, tooth by tooth, I pull down his zip very slowly.

I see nothing else but what I am waiting to see. He groans tries to interfere and I slap his hand. Feel his body relax. I burrow dig in deep for his balls and bring it all out in the palm of my hand like a shy sleeping animal into the night air.

I lean back on my heels to look.

He grows before my eyes, puffing out swelling dipping down then rising up higher, flailing blindly in the strange cold air. I want to caress it calm it

I want to torment it this broad stubby cock of his. I lean in and kiss the tip of it the blind-eye slit very lightly lots of little kisses. Then I lift his cock up tongue my way down to the base and open my mouth for one of his balls suck one of his pearl-shaped balls through the skin and sparse hair while I find the right grip for my hand around his cock. I make sure to take the other ball in my mouth also before I lean back again. I need to moisten him.

Gather the spittle on my tongue lick my tongue back up to the tip and plunge it deep into my throat in one go right in so that his body stiffens and I hear the metal door rattling again.

I find myself imagining what somebody passing the end of the lane might think they see down there in the shadows. Hoping.

A man, two men who decide to come down for a closer look…

As soon as he is wet enough, I close my hand firmly around his cock and push the skin right back and then roll it forward, gradually quickening the movement of my wrist until I could be pounding repeatedly on a door

let me in let me in now now

tickling flicking at the head of him with the tip of my tongue

suddenly swallowing it all the whole length of it to surprise him to hear him gasp.

I love this cock for being at my mercy. It needs my pity and my love or it is nothing. I want to hear its sorrowful song deep in my belly. This force that always wants to die. My knees sink deeper in the muck, scratched and bleeding.

He is moaning and so am I now. There is a thin tendon of skin I am tickling with my tongue on the underside that he seems to like a lot.

I reach for one of his hands and place it on my head

show him I want him to push my face my nose bury himself as deep as he can in my open mouth when he comes

he uses both hands fucks my beautiful mouth with his spasms so that I can't breathe and the warm jets of sperm splash at the back of my throat and still he doesn't let go and I think I have blacked out I'm choking can't swallow it down there's too much of it

there is nothing but this restriction the choking

and then I am gasping on my knees in the lane spitting it out swallowing and he is banging on the metal door with his fists howling with pleasure

roaring the whole city must hear it

YES, THE CITY NEEDS ME. I must have told him that I would see him later and hurried into the city centre, following the darkest streets, this city of old melancholy streets with a callous heart of gaudy glass. The seagulls circling like the world is falling silently from under us.

The seagulls make me open. The lonely call of the seagulls above the lights, swooping below the lights and always changing their minds. Where are you. Why did you leave me. I knew you would leave me. Their lament above the greedy streets. They make me open.

I'm opening.

His wad, he called it. I used to lie in the stale grass by the stream, the sharp reeds, the broken branches the brambles the thick green-skinned water so vulnerable the trees tried to protect it. I let the boys whip me. I used to pretend I was a statue toppled over in the grass by the river. It drove them mad. They would take off their clothes, tear them off and run around shouting screaming through the trees in total confusion. Whipping the trees with the twigs they peeled with their teeth. Digging holes in the ground with their hands. One boy put his hand into the wasps' nest for me.

I walk the streets in my long coat stained at the knees. My face stained at the mouth. I simply want something to happen. I am waiting for the pair of eyes that lives with the knowledge there is no proof to be found anywhere, no secret trace

no hidden face

Only in the dream are we real.

Take my arm all you brave men. I am a queen come down from her castle on the hill who wants to wrap herself in the magical twinkling shawl of earthly lights. I want to be doomed. I undo my belt and let my coat blow out behind me

the silk clings tighter to my skin like a lie.

Come forward the brave ones out of the shallow shadows.

He has eyes like the sun on a wet slate roof. Says he lives nearby, that he has a delicious wine to drink and some pictures I might like to see. He shows me his hands and tells me he was brought up on a farm near the sea. Will he taste of salt I wonder. Will he sting me. Tells me he has been wandering. That all he has learned is how to lie. He will be a good lover then, I decide, and slip my arm into his

like seaweed around a corpse.

He wants me naked immediately. I take off my coat and my dress and lie on the floor. Through the balcony doors I can see the glass arch I thought was some kind of threshold. While I was following the man I thought was Martin

thought was him thought was you. The face in the sky. I lie on the floor and he brings wine and books of erotic photographs for me to look at. He chops up his white powder with a razor blade on a glass table. I roll over on my back

over on my back and pull the ice bucket between my legs right up so it can go no further.

He wants to try on my dress. I put lipstick on his mouth. He walks around me sauntering pouting in my shoes and dress. I put my hand up inside his dress. He is hard. The thought of him coming against the lining of my dress makes me

He stands above me, his ankles tight against my shoulders, the dress pulled up to his navel. He is lean and muscular and probably shaves. I know by the look of him that

he has that look he can fuck me for hours whenever he feels like it this boy half my age in my silk dress drinking from a wine bottle and pouring it over me.

He says he bets my husband doesn't know the half of it does he and I let him think it because it clearly turns him on and he squats over me and starts to wank himself near my face

we do a line off the breasts of a laughing woman sitting on the shoulders of a statue, a goat man statue with horns

then he saunters around the room again, turns up the music

stands against the wall lifts up his skirt and lets it rest on his upright cock standing there pouting. He wants to dance for me.

I feel hollow the more he dances. A sadness unwinding through me, a terrible urgent loneliness. He wants to prance and talk and show off his cock. Out on the balcony where I go weeping to gaze at the brave lights of the city

searching for a shape in the lights a sign a face the mystic watermark

is this the real place am I real

die it tells me change always change die and change and dance and laugh forever and forever the city is telling me

where I am standing, leaning on the rail, so excited by this I feel I could burst, I start to pee and suddenly there he is ducking his head between my legs drinking clamps his open mouth around me. He is delirious, drunk and completely dazed.

I put him in a chair lift his dress and sit on him. Stroke his head like a child as I push against him.

this boy who

put his hand into the wasps for me, it was one summer, maybe the only summer we had a holiday together as a family. I didn't want to go. I had a new boyfriend and I was crazy about him and the things we did together. He promised he would write to me to our cottage in the west. I woke early every morning to be the first to the postbox, a white wooden box on a pole at the end of the lane. For days there was nothing and then one morning when I ran down the lane I saw that a swarm of wasps had settled on the box. I cried my eyes out until a boy came along. He was older than me with a crafty smile and a thousand jokes while he tortured me. I had seen him before. I promised him anything to look in the box for my letter.

Nothing is complete, Martin was always saying, not us, not God, not nature, not even what I'm trying to say now. My blue-eyed love and all your sweet useless words. My cowardly love. Your death comes to visit as a drugged boy in my black silk dress his stomach bloated with drinking gulping me

pissing up inside me with the pressure of me on top of him coming and the shameless lights of the city raining down on you in a thousand faces

my blood hardening in the hair of Donal's groin my love
my love hardening into a thousand statues on the horizon
Love is the great war to come.

ALMOST AS SOON AS I STEP back outside into the night, the limousine pulls in to the pavement. The door opens like a curtain parting, a black satin curtain in a dream, a trap, the crook of a lover's arm, like a sheet lifted to invite me into bed, like a sudden confession, like a wound, a mysterious jewellery box, the pocket of a coat, like an animal in my path, like what I deserve, a coffin lid, a glossy pinion, a lethal flower, a black cocoon, a black shell to press to my ear, a cave of black mineral, a compact with a black mirror, like something breaking silently snapping, like a shadow of what is behind me, a shadow on black water, a mouth, a pit, like the door of a washing machine, the window shutter of a sinister palace, a beckoning finger for obscene me, innocent me, like the paw of a fox, like love like what I have dreamed, and I bend my white elegant neck feel my breasts fall forward and climb in.

He is not there, we have to drive to where he is waiting. The driver's eyes flitting in and out of the mirror between the fixed square heads of the two front seats. I try to relax. I sense it will be a long journey, with the risk of danger. I had forgotten the danger. There are so many who want to stop us. The streets are deserted, the darkness pressed around the buildings like putty. A bump in the road brings on the warm trickle leaking from inside me and I have to clench my thighs and buttocks. To hide my own smell, I tuck a blanket tightly around me.

blanket has the smell of

HE IS THERE. We don't say a word as the car pulls out into the other traffic. We don't even look at each other yet. I face straight ahead. I am breathing heavily panting as if I've been running and I can't catch my breath properly and I am laughing all at the same time. They couldn't catch me. I have lost a shoe. I take off the other one and throw it out the window. The smell of oranges blows into the car through the open window, oranges turning blue. We pass the foundation stone and then a beautiful island of white grassy mould appears before us in the street. I roll up the window quickly. The driver accelerates; nothing separates us from the driver but he seems very far away, his bald wrinkled head above the seat frightens terrifies me—there is something wrong; he is missing his hat. The other one's eyes are red. I scream. This is not my car.

the door opens and I fall out

He is there. He takes my hand and slides me toward him across the seat. His soft hat has a wide uneven brim. He has a scar on his cheek, a recent scar. His lips are incredibly thick and sharply ridged but even so his mouth is bitter, lustful and bitter. He gloats over me with his storm green eyes. I notice he is in his bare feet, very hairy feet, and there is a thin silver bracelet around each ankle. Ramming his hand in between my thighs, he lifts me towards him on top of him and I am dribbling out all over him.

HE IS THERE but I can't see him in the dark interior, only his silhouette, only the occasional glimpse of him in the passing lights. I know I'm not allowed to stare at him. Or touch him. It is incredibly quiet inside the car; we are sealed off from the noise of the streets beyond the glass where there are all kinds of bizarre and violent scenes happening, people in the nude, fires, crowds looting, people having sex everywhere, bleeding faces. They spit against the windows. They piss at us. The car speeds through the chaos.

As deftly as possible, I wriggle out of my coat. The car fills with a smell like wet trees and I blush. He makes no mention of it, doesn't move a muscle. I can still taste the harsh white powder at the back of my throat, and between my legs. Perhaps to attract some attention to myself, I draw a big X on the windscreen with my lipstick as we pass over the bridge and the water red and steaming and full of people who will never go home again.

It is so solemn inside the car. I know there is a lot depending on me. He holds my hand tightly, for his own comfort. He is sad and I would do anything to take it away from him. I want him to put his face between my legs and inhale me choke those sighs of his. The car stops on an old cobbled street. He leaves me alone with the driver who only stares at me in the mirror, too far away for me to read his expression. There is a terrible foul smell I can't name. I have to hold my breath not to puke.

takes me up wooden stairs to a landing. Three men are whispering outside a door; they kneel as I am brought towards them. A single candle burns in an extravagant golden candelabra balanced on a stool.

He puts his hands on my shoulders gazes into my eyes as though for the last time.

One of the men leads me into the room. It is bare and cold. There is rubbish pushed into a corner. It is dark. One wall has a hole in it, the bricks smashed out, right in the middle of a hideous picture somebody was drawing smearing there in blood and faeces. The floorboards creak.

I am ushered closer to the bed where they have a frail old man laid out.

He is wheezing sick, about to die maybe, that's what I'm thinking, and what they expect of me, why they have brought me to his side and then he begins to open his eyes the slowest sweetness wonder like a dawn

and smiles at me so warmly

potently so loving

that I understand and I am flooded my body made rich with joy.

I slide the straps off my shoulders let my dress fall around me in the dust.

AN OLD WOMAN WASHES ME FIRST. She puts her fingers into every orifice, every crack and hollow. She combs my hair, pinches my cheeks. From tiny golden pots with the most delicate spouts, she rubs ointments into my skin that smell like nothing I've ever known, richer than any flower or spice, older, sweeter, instantly invigorating every pore and nerve in my body. She braids some of my hair with pearls.

I am brought into a room full of men and

I am brought into a bedroom. I have to pee immediately. So much pours out of me that I am almost frightened. Afterwards, as I look at myself in the mirror, I see the open bathroom door behind me, the square of soft carpet in lamplight, the ugly chair and the corner of a strange bed. This is a place I have dreamed about. Frantic, I see the plant with the waxy flower like a yellow lily in a pot in the bathtub. I understand suddenly that I am in a hotel room.

and the room will be full of smoke and the men's voices will subside as I am led in laid out on the bed.

A sad young boy in a purple robe comes into the bathroom carrying a stool. He sets it down behind me stands up on it his hands on my bare shoulders. He ties the blood stained ultramarine blindfold over my eyes.

I'm terrified.

I don't know how many of them there are.

To begin with, I have to make myself come for them.

for him

because I know he is there among them watching with pride.

And I know that the cock that grazes my lips is his and the cock at my ear and the hands under my buttocks opening my knees and in the silence after I have come for them shown them my glory and heard their feet shuffling across the carpet the door closing the mouth at my so long painful nipples the cock that goes up inside me is his and as I come again and again he won't be able to resist, he'll pull off the blindfold and kiss my eyes his treasure

and then I can really begin. Then I am ready at last only then. My hunger is born. I peel away a thousand times. The hunger he wants. I have to take him lead him. The world of dust crumbles away as I sit on him. He is calling to me to bring him with me. I am dripping gushing screaming splitting igniting destroying riding. The trees fall away

the trees are the markers others have left to show how far they came

they fall away their huge ugly roots trying to grab me tearing the skin off me lashing me

I can't stop I am barely even a memory of my own vagina raw and boiling hunger

come with me my love

my vagina to kiss the lips of

the infinite walls of my vagina

up ahead there is a glorious runny vastness

THE DRIVER IS NOT ALLOWED to touch me. At midnight I come down the steps in my robe which he takes from me along with my slippers and I get into the back of the car. We drive through the country roads, twisting narrow roads, the trees bushes houses appearing starkly in the white headlights like warnings, dangers, reproofs, until we reach the turn for the motorway. There, he parks the car by a broken five bar gate and moves into the back with me. It is our secret. I lie on the floor and let him take me. He doesn't want much, to empty himself into me only, always the same steady rhythm. I kiss him gently lightly lots of them the way he likes. When he's finished he wipes his huge old man's cock with a pressed handkerchief and gives me a wink. Then we drive onto the motorway speed towards the city.

the streaming showers of red and white lights going different ways always entrances me turns me on their lonely separation the barrier

no touching until we enter the city.

Sometimes I ask the driver questions about himself, about his wife and family. Whether he has had a happy life. What he has learned about love. Or I talk to him about myself. Tonight I want to tell him about the wasp boy.

I don't remember his name anymore but I begged him to help me discover if there was a letter in the box. The first morning he kissed me and made me take off my T-shirt to look at my young breasts as though he were the first ever. The second morning he took off my knickers and made me rub him outside his trousers and he came quickly shuddering afraid like he didn't know what was happening to him. He dragged me into the trees and stripped me naked on the third morning. I was sure he had been awake through the night planning it. He was getting more confident, more specific. The moist spongy ground, the delicate breaths of mist among the old trees, the grotesque boils of sap splitting the bark, enormous dewy cobwebs sprinkled with pine needles and high in the branches vivid green shawls of moss blocking out the sky—he didn't notice any of this, only my young white startling skin.

and his desire to hurt it

and the noises he was driven to hear me make.

He had a new position for me every morning, a new series of investigations of my body, new implements twigs stones thorns his penknife his belt his teeth

The shadows swelled like damp under his eyes and he spoke less and less. Mushroom eyes.

The morning he decided to piss on me everything was wet after a night of rain. The idea came to him suddenly—he was already hidden behind a tree. I watched him running toward me, like he was afraid he would change his mind, covering himself with both hands, and he wouldn't look at me as he aimed it down across my stomach which was covered in leaves and soil

or when he took a switch to my bum and shepherded me deeper into the wood on my hands and knees

or the day he lit a cigarette and stuck the burning tip into his own palm as a way to prove show something to me and I scooped his soft bloody penis into my mouth

the smell of flesh and pine and semen

the whipping

a fox in the mist we both chased naked

the day he wept and ran off

and the day we broke into a cottage and dressed up in their clothes and he pretended to be his limping father and I was my mother sick in the bed and he went inside me and I came with him for the first time.

Did you ever get a letter then? the driver wants to know.

Nothing, I tell him. The wasps left after a week but we continued to meet. Every morning before anyone was awake. Then one morning he brought me a gift emptied his pockets out on the top of a rock. Necklaces and bracelets and rings and chains and earrings in a glittering knotted pile on the mossy rock. I guessed he must have stolen them. He was so proud of his offering. Kissing him, I put both my hands down inside his trousers. It dawned on me then he was saying goodbye to me. That was the first time I was angry with him in spite of everything he had done. I slapped his face. As usual I had forgotten it would have to end.

Nothing ever ends, the driver says merrily and at the same moment we can see the city platter below us through the windscreen like it is a steaming bleeding carcass just skinned

the entrails of lights like nerves knots of muscle rind

pools of fat giblets

we should be able to tell the future from this mess of guts and bones

a treasure trove tangle of smouldering jewels and gossamer chains for the stone giantess

The first one we spot is outside a nightclub. He gets into the back without hesitation. He's excited, can't believe his luck. A beautiful naked woman in the back of a limousine. I am meant to sit still like a statue and talk to no one. He slides across to me stares at my breasts rapturously. He kisses my shoulder but he gets no response. The car stops again. This time it's a woman's voice I hear. She's suspicious, abusive to the driver. He is unperturbed. I have listened to him convince the most reluctant virgins that they will always regret not opening the door. He believes completely in the power of the sight of me on the back seat, luscious, nude, cold. And this time he is successful again, and the woman climbs in. She is small, a teenage figure with a disappointed older face, sits with her arms folded. The young man tries to amuse her. We drive around for quite a while before the driver slows again for what sounds like a couple. This time however he fails to persuade them. The streets at this time of night remind me of underground tunnels, of the dreams I had in the concrete pipes I lay down in as a girl, my skirt around my hips, a boy fumbling on top of me. Sometimes we turn into a street and have to slow down because of the seagulls searching angrily among the rubbish, not for food I like to imagine, for something else they've lost a long time ago, the source of their lament. We are stopping again. Another man gets in. He is very handsome wears a fisherman's cap. He takes his place comfortably, as if he knows already what's ahead, as if he's heard the rumours of the black limo. He is content for the moment to admire me and wait. We drive on. By the time we leave the city there are seven of us in the car.

He will have everything ready by the time we reach the house again.

THE FIRST ONE WE SPOT is outside a nightclub. The driver hasn't even finished making his offer before the door opens and a young man is grinning at me, looking me up and down. As soon as he sits in, I get on my knees between his legs and open him bring him out into my mouth and suck him. Before I've finished the car has stopped again and I hear the driver talking to somebody else. It is a woman this time. She is suspicious, abusive. The driver is unperturbed. As my throat fills with this strange young man's semen, the door opens and she takes in the scene, a naked woman between a man's legs. She laughs with delight and gets in, hurriedly getting out of her dress. Next there is another man with a sad face who all three of us go to work on. Within an hour the car is crowded with twisting naked bodies. The seats and carpet are slippery with semen and there's blood from biting smeared on the windows.

We are not so lucky every night. The driver has taken me back alone some nights, or alone with an hysterical girl who has changed her mind or some drunken man who has fallen asleep with his cock in his hands and me laid out on the floor for him wearing only my pearls. We drive into the city late at night after the bars and clubs have shut and collect the spellbound ones who don't want to wake up. We take them out to the house. They can stay as long as they want.

I wonder what he will say when he finds out we were not able to restrain control ourselves. He will be waiting at the top of the steps for the sight of the headlights sweeping through the trees.

THERE MUST HAVE BEEN A CRASH. In the midst of the orgy, we didn't hear the driver shouting to us or the brakes screeching. The car skidded on the black ice without us even noticing, smashed through the barrier into the opposite lanes. I had two cocks in my mouth and one up inside me

was lost in scuttling rapid wave after wave of pleasure when we hit the other car flipped over

and the glass tore and the metal shattered and the screams twisted and disembowelled everyone of them.

There were bodies all over the road. I still wasn't sure what had happened.

Smeared with blood, I began to crawl blindly across the broken glass. My pearls were pressed deep into my skin like scalding seeds. The moon wanted to suck them out. My hair was smoking.

I crawled into the fog where I thought it would cool me and protect me. They would find me in the morning frozen like a statue by the side of the road and wonder who I was.

A bloody statue. I knew I had become love itself as I crawled along the motorway in the dark. I am love, I said to myself over and over again. My injured nakedness was my message. My embedded necklace was my mystery. At the same time, I had the feeling there were cars driving by me, unable to even see me. Their headlights passed over my skin like a child's gaze, entire cars passed right through me. The fog kept moving further away, a figure in it, maybe more than one, wanting me to follow.

Then, all of a sudden

I was picked up lifted up scooped off the ground in one powerful jolt.

I was hanging upside down.

the wrong way up like love.

being carried at an incredible speed swinging the wrong way up

like love.

My face bumping against a carpet I thought but underneath the carpet had to be muscle, deep compressed thick bulging rippling regions of muscle.

Something was carrying me, leaping with me hung over its shoulder across hedges roads rivers over the tops of the trees.

My dangling arms brushed against what had to be an enormous tail of intoxicating softness that soothed the pain.

I crawled up its back, using the last of my strength, swung my legs around its neck

held on with my thighs

held on with my hands to its huge pointed ears the horns

bounding over the houses the trees my face in the stars

bleeding love taken back to where she belongs.